Contents

Acknowledgments

ACKNOWLEDGEMENTS

From flash fiction prompt to collaborative web serial to this book, so many people have helped us make this book a reality. We both want to specifically thank writer, editor, contributor and all-around great person, Cindy Vaskova for her innumerous contributions to this story along the way.

Fellow writers and friends L. Fergus and Meg MacDonald helped us whip the final draft into shape. Everyone who assisted but didn't get a shout out here, we didn't forget about you, we just ran out of space on this page. Thank you so much for all your help.

And finally, thank you, reader. We appreciate you taking the time to read our humble scribbling on our blogs and in this story.

"*S*ire, may I see it?"

"The Automaton?" the king sighed. "You've seen it before, Jarvis."

"Yes Mi'Lord, I ask only to allow a young artisan to sketch it. We may learn to augment the infirm."

The king rose from his desk and turned his attention to Jarvis. "Do you believe that wise?"

"Mi'Lord, she destroyed the automaton."

The king looked over Jarvis' shoulder. "Where is Snow?"

"Mi'Lady is supervising construction of an orphanage in the northern reach of the kingdom," replied Jarvis.

"She is not to know about it. Ensure your artisan knows the penalty for defying me."

Jarvis nodded first to the king, and then to a royal guard. The guard opened one of the ornate doors, and a young woman entered. The trio walked to a stone wall off of the throne room. The king withdrew an apple made of solid gold and placed it in an ornamental set of scales on a pedestal prominently displayed against the wall. Its purpose was to be a symbol of the king's fairness when resolving conflicts among his people.

The artisan's eyes grew as the apple weighted one side and, as the tray sank, an audible click echoed off the tall ceiling. A section of wall slid aside, brass wheels squeaked as they revealed earthen steps leading down into the very mountain the castle was built upon.

After Jarvis and the artisan had disappeared down the steps, the king removed the apple and watched as the wall restored itself. He returned to his desk and removed a fragment of glass from a hidden drawer. He held the broken glass fragment up, staring at his reflection, the edges rough as if it had been smashed from a larger piece.

"Magic mirror in my hand..."

The fragment's reflection began to cloud, and a blurry face materialized. Tendrils of magick materialized over the king's reflection. "Master?" the replacement face asked.

"Let me know when Snow returns to the castle."

"It is done," the magical mirrored face responded.

"Show me the automaton's chamber."

The face faded, and the king's reflection morphed into a view of an earthen chamber, its details blocked from view by the artisan's pale features. Her lips moved, but no sound came from the glass fragment. The king leaned the fragment against a leather-bound book and his eyes repeatedly darted to it as he tried to complete paperwork.

~

"Is this...?"

"It is," Jarvis replied. "The mirror was cracked into seven fragments when the evil queen hurled a goblet at it. His Majesty is undoubtedly watching us from another fragment."

The artisan glanced furtively at the glass fragment as Jarvis inserted a key into a simple wooden door, and threw it open. Past the door frame was a brass clockwork automaton. It stood six feet, the brass components reflecting light from a surface so perfect, it couldn't have been forged in this or any other kingdom that the artisan knew of. It perfectly mimicked the human body with bones and muscle. The only thing missing was the head and right arm. Where they would've been ended in mangled metal.

The artisan reached toward the automaton and jerked her hand away when she heard grinding metal.

Jarvis let out a belly laugh and dropped a piece of brass to the floor as the artisan whirled toward him. He stepped away from the wall where he had scratched it with the brass.

"Forgive me, young artisan, it's sort of a tradition when someone sees it for the first time."

The artisan let out a breath. "I thought it was alive."

Jarvis exhaled his own breath, the mischievous smile faded from his lips. His features became a shadow, and a morose frown replaced his fading smile. "It was," he whispered.

The artisan raised her eyebrows and tilted her head.

"What you see here is a killing machine," Jarvis continued.

"A killing machine?"

"It can't be bargained with. It can't be reasoned with. It doesn't feel pity, or remorse, or fear. And it absolutely will not stop, ever, until its target is dead."

The artisan stepped away from the automaton. "Who was its target?"

Jarvis leaned against the wall. "His Majesty was the target."

The artisan stepped back again and nearly tripped over the door jamb.

Jarvis sighed. "I'll tell you a story, but you will never repeat it. Especially not to the queen."

The artisan nodded conspiratorially.

"What's your name, girl?"

The artisan swallowed a lump in her throat. "Sarah."

"Well, Sarah, this story happened when his majesty was still a young boy, a huntsman to be precise. It's the story of a clockwork machine from the future, with a mission to terminate his Majesty to prevent him from meeting his queen." Jarvis paused for effect. "Queen White."

Sarah sat on the earthen floor mute and waited for Jarvis to continue.

~

"JOHN!" THE VOICE ECHOED OFF NEARBY TREES. "JOHN!"

John looked up and skittered away from his tutor. He moved continuously, to keep the pigs and their mud between them.

"You're late for your studies," his tutor declared, crossing her arms over her chest.

John moved again as the tutor circled the pig pen. "I've decided I'm not studying today," he announced.

The tutor examined the distance between them. "I shall inform your father of your decision."

John stopped circling the pen, and a smile crept across his lips as the tutor turned to leave. The tutor spun and leaped over the pigs, landing in the mud and splattering John with pig filth. John reeled back and fell on his back. She jumped again and crashed against John as he sputtered about the indignity of the situation. She knelt with one knee on John's chest.

Leaning forward, she whispered into John's ear. "I've been watching you for many years, and the time is near."

"Time..." John squirmed under her knee. "Time for what?"

"The beginning," the tutor whispered. She shrugged emphatically and continued, "The end."

"What are you blathering about, Reese?"

"The evil queen," Reese replied matter-of-factly.

"What evil queen?"

"The evil queen who will cast a spell on your wife."

"Are you stupid, woman? I'm not married."

"You will be." Reese stared at the surrounding forest. Birds scattered from the canopy as a crashing noise was heard. Lightning flashed repeatedly and started small fires in the underbrush. Something large was advancing toward them.

John stared as wildlife thundered frantically from the bushes. "They're terrified," he screamed to Reese.

With steam escaping from articulating joints, a gleaming brass man emerged from shadows along the tree line. Clockwork parts were partially visible behind its brass chest plate. The automaton tore a tree trunk from the ground, roots littering clumps of soil, and launched the tree like a javelin. Reese pushed John out of the way, barely avoided the projectile herself.

John scrambled back on all fours and stared up at Reese's outstretched hand. Reese met John's gaze and she uttered the words that would start an adventure through time and tale, "Come with me if you want to live."

~

"MIRRORED FRAGMENT IN MY HAND, SHOW ME NOW THE brass-made man."

The glass fragment reflected the old woman's withered features. Her visage slowly faded, and all that was left was her floating smile. The smile morphed until tendrils weaved and bobbed in the mirror. After a moment, an androgynous face replaced them. The face's lips were peeling and the facial features were cracked. Eyes empty of light stared back at the old woman. The disembodied head attenuated and rippled as it was replaced by a rolling forest.

"There it is!" she crooned.

The glass fragment showed a man made of brass uproot a tree and launch it at two cowering figures. One was covered in mud and pig excrement, while the other stood defiant against what she saw. The old woman had to move the glass fragment to follow the action. The figures dove out of the way, the tree barely striking one. The brass automaton's clockwork gears propelled it forward in a leap, and a burst of steam arrested its decent.

"What have you got there, prisoner?" A guard banged the hilt of his sword on the bars to the woman's cell.

The withered woman secreted the glass fragment in

her tattered robe and turned to face the guard. "I have nothing," she croaked.

"I saw you with something," the guard retorted.

The crone extended her arms and spun in a circle, gesturing around the room. "I've been locked in this cell for generations," she rasped. "The oracle foresaw my death in this very cell."

The guard stepped back, but still attempted to project an air of authority. His eyes narrowed into slits as he surveyed the woman older than the castle and the kingdom he had vowed to protect. He leaned against the wall, still facing her, but he let his eyes fall slack. The woman withdrew her hands into her robe and ran a callused thumb against the rough edge of the glass fragment. The guard missed the slight wince as the glass drank from her bloody thumb.

 ∽

"COME WITH ME IF YOU WANT TO LIVE!"

John looked back at the brass automaton, the escaping steam bending grass and its feet sinking into the soft topsoil. John lunged and gripped Reese's outstretched hand with his own. She hauled him to his feet as a high-pitched whine escaped the brass automaton.

"It needs to build up pressure before it can attack again!" Reese shouted as she dragged John away from his farm and the menace of whirling gears and dark magick.

John looked forlornly at the pigs screeching in the mud. He doubted that they would survive the wrath of the brass monstrosity. "We have to get to the castle," he yelled as he stumbled after Reese.

Reese looked over her shoulder just long enough to ensure John was following. "The soldiers of this time are not equipped to handle something like this."

"And you can?"

"With the weapons of the time? I don't know."

"Time?"

"Don't worry about it right now."

John skidded to a stop. "You'll tell me now!"

Reese doubled back to where John obstinately stood, her shoulders square with irritation. She seized John by the neck and spun him toward the brass automaton. "Do you see that thing?" she shouted into his ear. "That thing will kill you."

"Why me?"

"I told you, it wants to prevent you from meeting your wife."

John struggled from her grip. "And I told you, 'I'm not married!'"

Reese rolled her eyes and pulled on John's arm. "An evil queen wants to kill a beautiful princess. She's the fairest in the land."

Reese kept looking back to the automaton in the distance as they ran away. "The evil queen will hire you to kill the princess."

John slowed at the revelation. "I won't kill anyone."

"I know this." Reese sighed and gazed at the automaton as it shrank in the distance. "But the evil queen doesn't. You only pretended to kill the princess, and the evil queen cast a spell on her causing her to fall into a deep sleep. You will wake her with a kiss, and you will be her king."

John and Reese staggered into a stable and began saddling a pair of horses.

"Why is the automaton trying to kill me?"

"Don't you see?" Reese grumbled as she tightened a strap on the horse. "If you don't wake the princess, the evil queen will reign, and the world will crumble to her gruesome whim."

The duo rode out of the stable as an increasing pitch from the brass automaton finally ceased. The automaton's clockwork eyes moved, the glass fragments reflecting the scene of its escaping targets.

∽

THE OLD WOMAN SCORED THE BACK OF HER GLASS fragment against the stonework as her guard snored loudly in the hallway. She snapped a small piece off the larger fragment, rubbing it against the wall, and repositioning it time and time again until the glass started to become round. She smiled and pushed the small pile of glass dust around with her dirty bare foot until it was indistinguishable from the dirt that accompanied her cell. She held up a second round glass fragment, comparing the two pieces, and smiled again at her progress.

∽

SARAH WATCHED THE ODD UP-SIDE-DOWN IMAGE FROM

the glass fragment Jarvis handed her. The old crone finished grinding the glass pieces to match, hid them in her robes, and settled in to sleep for the night. Sarah handed the fragment back to Jarvis and turned toward the brass automaton.

"Can I touch it?" she asked.

"Yes, but do not touch the mangled metal, it is sharp where it was crushed, and it feeds on blood."

Sarah jerked her hand away but still walked around the pedestal examining the defunct automaton. "How did its head and arm get crushed?"

Jarvis smiled and replied, "That would be skipping ahead to the end of the tale."

Sarah nodded and sat back on the stonework in silent respect as the enigmatic Jarvis continued to tell the story. The king watched them both from his own glass fragment and felt the weight of the story as it unfolded in the hidden room below.

*J*ohn laid in the hay feeling more exhausted than he ever had before. He wasn't sure he could move again even if the brass automaton burst through the barn wall. He looked uneasily at the barn wall again, uncertain just how much probability there was in his errant thought. Reese seemed to read as mind, and said, "We should be safe here for the night. If nothing else we likely forced it to feed."

John remembered something about it feeding on blood, and thought better of asking for further details. He had only ever known Reese as his tutor, but she was like a knight of the realm jumping off the page and into the flesh.

"How did you know there would be quicksand in the clearing?" John finally asked. The weight of their second close escape ran through his mind over and over again.

"I put it there," she answered simply, before dashing up the ladder to recheck the barn's loft.

He followed her with his eyes. "But, then why didn't he follow us around the edge of the clearing?"

Reese kicked a pile of hay down on him and with a smile replied, "Because it always follows in a straight line."

John blinked as he processed her statement. "And what about the-"

"You ask a lot of questions, John," she interrupted in a firm voice. "Maybe you should be resting."

"And that's another thing," he insisted. "How are you still so energetic? Especially since you're a-" John stopped talking as abruptly as she had stopped moving, gulping at her stare.

"Only a woman?" she asked quietly.

"Well..." John answered, suddenly taking a keen interest in a course strand of hay.

Reese threw up her arms, let out an exasperated sigh, and climbed down the ladder. "Fine," she said in a huff, "after all, it's you it wants to kill, not me. I guess you've earned the full story."

John realized it had only been a matter of hours since he had demanded to know that story. Now the thought of it turned his stomach.

Reese snorted at his discomfort before starting, "Decades hence, the evil queen will not yet be a queen, but she will have given herself wholly to evil magick. She came to the castle in the guise of an old crone during a time of wary peace. We had been at war with our neighbors, the Rookskye, for generations. We didn't so much have a truce with them, as that all their border incursions simply stopped.

"The main connector to our countries was The Bridge, spanning the deep, and cold, Allooashinn River. For three years no one from Rookskye had come over it, and no from Oossah who dared to cross had ever returned. No one that is, until she came across, appearing out of the fog on a sickly mare. It collapsed under her as soon as it reached Oossah soil, and she begged the guards for aid. Soon enough she was telling her story in the Capitol to the Council of Nine."

John thought he heard a faint rustling outside, but he brushed it off as one of the farm animals. The brass automaton was many things, but quiet was not one of them, and he was enraptured by Reese's tale.

"She had a silver hand mirror with her, which one of the Council of Nine identified as belonging to the Rookskye royal family. She claimed to have been one of the royal nannies, and, even more shocking the only surviving Rookskye left!"

"You mean of the royal house, don't you?" asked John incredulously.

"No, of all the Rookskye. She described in detail the Oossah magical mirror, and then showed them that the silver hand mirror was of similar magick."

"But the magic mirror was shattered centuries ago! Only seven fragments still survive."

"Magick obeys no law save its own. Not even time. The mirror of legend during this time is yet whole. It's not until it's later shattered that the breaking spans through all of time."

"But-" John stuttered. "That is-" he failed again to form a coherent sentence.

"Don't," Reese demanded, "it just is." Her stern face softened. "Whether it makes sense to any save magick matters not."

John shook his head and pondered Reese's statement. He wondered just how many animals the farm must have when he heard more shuffling outside. Reese continued, her eyes looking up in remembrance, "She showed an invading horde in the mirror. The Tenyks. Once men, twisted by dark magick into slavering, bloodthirsty savages, closer in mind to beasts than man."

"The council panicked, of course, as they recognized the magnitude of the threat. They could clearly see in the mirror that the Tenyks were mere days away from Oossah. They knew there was not enough time for them to marshal the countryside and ready defenders before the evil horde arrived. So, when the crone offered them a solution, they leapt for it.

"They took her to the magic mirror where she used her magick to connect to every reflection throughout the land. Whether it was a mirror, still water, or a shiny blade, her visage was seen. Just as she was about to call every male in Oossah to arms, her form changed before the Council of Nine's eyes. She raised from her stoop, her warts and lesions gave way to smooth, unblemished skin, and the years melted away from her face until it was beautiful beyond compare."

"Every man in the room fell into a dark swoon for her, as did every man in all of Oossah who saw her reflection. Their wills became lost in their darkened lust for her beauty, and she easily added them to her army."

"She had an army, too?" asked John, feeling even more fright.

"Of course," replied Reese, cocking her head, "Who else would the Tenyks be?"

Before John could answer the door and windows to the barn burst open, giving way to snarling, mindless men in mismatched black armor.

"Tenyks!" Reese shouted, "Quick John, to the loft!"

∽

JOHN STARED AT THE TENYKS LAYING FLAT ON HIS BACK. There were at least a dozen more forever trapped in the contorted positions in which they died. The Tenyks on the Barn floor were different though, and John couldn't take his eyes away from the agonized face struggling to move despite a broken back. It wasn't just that it was the only one still alive, it was that John had sent it to its current pain. He'd managed to cast it down from the loft when it had surprised him, interrupting his flight for refuge.

"How many more? Where?" Reese was demanding of the thing. "Tell me and I will end your suffering quickly." When her answer was naught but the silent movement of its lips like a fish gaping at its own reflection in a tank, Reese deftly slid her dagger across its throat. She shook her head and sighed before looking around the area.

The freezing of its face in a mask of impotent fury roused John to speak, "I don't believe it!"

"I know. This is bad. Very bad."

John scoffed at her nonchalance. "You killed a helpless man!" He steadied his legs against the loft ledge and prepared himself against the force of Reese's glare.

"Look at them John. How much humanity is left? When you wound a stag to where it cannot walk, do you wait for it to die slowly? Or do you end its suffering?"

John used the excuse of coming down from the loft to avoid answering. He looked at the Tenyks faces again, but closer this time. He looked beyond his horror and disgust. Even in death, there was a mark of humanity that remained with people. Here there was none. Their faces bore only the marks of savagery and the grim castings of hatred. "I'm sorry Reese, this is all so-" He paused and closed his eyes. "So-"

"Yeah," Reese replied with a sigh, "I know."

~

IT WAS SOME HOURS, AND MORE MILES THAN JOHN thought possible, before they spoke again. "Why is it so bad, Reese?" he finally asked.

Reese sighed, and her eyes focused far away before she answered. "Time is fickle even for magick. The evil queen made a time portal to send the brass automaton back to get you." Her eyes met his. "A rip in time itself," she added when she saw that he didn't understand. "I tried to stop it, but fell through it instead, arriving years before the brass automaton did. So, the Tenyks could only have come through if it was stabilized. Which would also mean many, many more of them."

"Oh," John replied, deflated.

"Our only hope is that we found out about it, and stopped it before any more could make it through."

"How would we do that?" asked John after some quiet, confused thinking.

"Not you and me, 'We,' my Sisters, 'We.' Bugger time and talking about it!" she added, kicking a small rock.

"How many Sisters do you have?"

Reese released a full, hearty laugh, one that John couldn't remember ever having heard from her before. "I have been trapped here so long I forget how little you know and how long ago it was. It has been a long time since I've truly thought of them. Hundreds, John, I have hundreds if not thousands of sisters."

"You have..."

"Thousands of sisters yes. It's what we call ourselves. Almost every man exposed to the evil queen's spell was trapped. Forever. There was nothing that we could do, and believe me we tried everything. Her spell was so powerful, so profound, that we were helpless. The women though, and most of the younger boys, were swayed but not controlled. When the evil queen's mirrored message ended, we broke free."

"There was only one woman on the Council of Nine, and she realized what was going on immediately. She made her escape through a secret passage and then organized the resistance. She gathered the Sisters, the boys, and those few men who weren't trapped, and brought them to the shelter of the caves.

"The eastern mountains are our home now. The men toil over our flocks and the few crops we can grow. The Sisters ensure that the evil queen is reminded of her mortality and that no Tenyks who enter the foothills leave alive."

She crouched suddenly, pulling John down with her. He strained to be quiet, even holding his breath tight enough to hear his own heartbeat in his ears. It sounded far too loud and fast.

"Breathe fool!" she hissed. "Just do it quietly."

He saw now what she had seen. It was a small village, though he couldn't remember ever visiting it. He wondered if it even had a name beyond, "The Village," for the surrounding people. Something about it felt profoundly wrong, though.

He couldn't quite place his reservations when Reese whispered, "The people are gone."

WARY OF TRAPS, IT TOOK THEM HOURS TO VERIFY THAT the village was indeed empty. On their final pass, Reese grinned, "There!"

"People?" John asked, looking in all directions.

"Better. A blacksmith shop. Now we may just stand a chance against the brass automaton. Then we can worry about the time portal."

Any questions John had about the plan were soon lost as she directed their preparations. "Do you think this will work, Reese?" he asked while they ate dry bread with their backs against the blacksmith's cold forge.

"I hope so. We don't have many options left, but at least it's a practical plan."

"It's just nice to not be running anymore," John added some time later after they finished their meager rations in silence.

"It is." She nodded and met his silent stare. "The more so when it's harder in some ways too."

"I've been thinking about the Sisters," he added, nodding to her sagacity. "Don't you worry that one of the men will catch a reflection somewhere and be turned while he's with you in the caves?"

"No, not anymore," she replied. "We take strict measures to ensure they can never see a reflection."

"Oh-" John started. "But, how would you even manage that?"

Reese took a long swallow from a wineskin they'd found before answering. "We blind them."

*E*scaping steam whistled, and the sound of breaking foliage echoed across the valley. John looked over his shoulder as the brass automaton crashed through the tree line. Light reflected from the monster's remaining eye blinded him. He raised his hand to block the light while staring down at it. Smiling, he turned to Reese, who didn't join him in his exuberance. John's eyes scanned her body. Like his, she was covered with bruises, cuts, and scrapes. Some were deep, and the tinge of scarlet on her tattered shirt told him how close to death they'd come since learning the secrets she had kept from him for so many years.

"You know what to do," Reese whispered.

John nodded stoically as the behemoth launched into the air. The arc was known; they'd battled it enough to know its limitations. Brass against stone, the noise was deafening. The duo watched as the automaton gathered steam pressure for another jump.

Reese allowed a smirk as she counted out the number of jumps. "One."

John turned and started to look further up the mountain.

"Don't look at it. The Queen's Assassin can still see you with its good eye."

John spun around, and although from his height he couldn't make out the mechanical face, he saw in his mind's eye the mount where the magic mirror fragment was attached. Reese seemed to know exactly where to set up their trap, and when the chopped log struck the monstrosity in the head, he thought his ordeal was through.

Another high pitched release and another crash into the rocky terrain. "Two," Reese whispered, the brass automaton got closer.

John could feel emotion radiate from Reese. *Our trap will work,* he thought, but he perceived an almost depressed feeling from Reese. He stared at her, but she turned away. *Something's not right,* he thought.

Reese met his gaze long enough to count out the next leap. "Three," she said.

The steam-powered whine reached a crescendo as Reese yelled out, "Now!"

John skittered behind a boulder, and Reese kicked away a wooden stump.

"Push, damn you!" The shout from his protector spurred him to action. John planted his feet against the earthen wall and pushed against the boulder with everything he had.

The impact from the brass man caused the ground to shudder and loose the boulder from its stony slumber. The hiss-click was heard over the rumbling of the boulder as the evil queen's construct attempted to leap from the path of the boulder, but there wasn't enough time for it to build up enough pressure. Tendrils of compressed gas leaked from its shattered arm.

The boulder struck the mechanical man in a glancing blow, but it was enough to throw the beast back. Once, twice, thrice the automaton tumbled end over end until it landed upside-down in a sturdy tree that had sprouted from the cliff face. When the boulder impacted the cliff with the automaton's head pinned between, a cacophony of sound erupted. Steam, brass, and rock fragments rained down on the mountainside, showering John and Reese with debris.

~

"CERIDWEN, MY QUEEN."

Ceridwen ignored the man who knelt before her brass throne. Instead, she kept her eyes affixed to the mirrored fragment as the events on the mountainside unfolded. She flinched as the boulder crushed the head of the clockwork automaton she had had painstakingly constructed by her loyal Tenyks.

She watched the eye of the automaton sail in a steep arc, propelled by a column of steam. From her bird's eye view, she saw a stone fragment strike Reese White in the chest before it tumbled out of view.

~

"REESE!"

John leaped over debris and ducked under falling ejecta. His eyes focused on the singular goal of reaching his fallen friend. He skidded to a stop on his knees and picked up Reese's broken body.

"Reese!" he yelled again, his vision blurred with tears. "Don't you die on me!"

Reese laid in his arms, and her chest shuddered, trying to take in air. She forced a smile between ragged breaths. "Tell mother I love her," she rasped as her entire body shook violently with the effort of speech.

John squeezed Reese's lifeless body to his chest, unashamed of his tears.

⁓

SARAH WIPED HER EYES WITH THE BACK OF HER HAND AND looked to the defunct brass automaton standing silently on the pedestal.

"What a sad story," she whispered.

"It gets worse," Jarvis replied. He handed her a goblet to drink.

"How?" she asked, as she drank the wine to steady her shaking fingers.

Jarvis picked up his staff in reply and wedged it in a deep crease where the shoulder blades would have been if the abomination were made of flesh and bone. He turned to Sarah and pointed to a dusty chest behind the platform. "Open the chest, and bring me the sack inside."

Sarah complied and lifted the burlap sack from the wooden chest. Metal clanked from within, and it caused her heart to race. Jarvis leaned against the staff and balanced his weight on one end. Sarah stared wide-eyed as the staff slowly lowered and an audible click echoed off the stone ceiling.

Sarah backed away as the dented chest plate split

open and revealed a hollow space inside. Telltale remnants of steam escaped as the arms and legs also opened revealing that they too were hollow.

Jarvis walked around the front of the machine, and Sarah followed.

"Ceridwen couldn't make this thing think."

Sarah nodded.

"She is the queen of dark magick."

"'Is'?" Sarah responded, her speech starting to slur.

Jarvis nodded, picked up the sack, and emptied its contents onto the stone floor. Brass shards tumbled and scattered. Sarah muttered, her lips failing to create the words. Jarvis lifted the young girl and placed her into the brass automaton. The openings closed on the artist, with only her neck, head, and left arm protruding from the metal sarcophagus.

Jarvis wrapped the burlap bag around a jagged brass piece and sliced Sarah's cheek. Blood dribbled, and as it coated the mangled brass, the pieces that were strewn on the floor began to rattle. They chased each other around the pedestal, the brass fragments rose until an unseen force placed each twisted metal piece over Sarah's exposed flesh.

Jarvis looked away and covered his ears to the shrieks of anguish from inside the metal cocoon.

～

"You have seen it?"

Snow's eyes focused on the Advancing figure. "Yes, Sky," she replied, pausing to keep her voice even. "We all make sacrifices to the cause."

"Reese will be remembered..."

Snow slammed the glass fragment down on her desk, and the impact caused a rough edge to cut her hand. "Damn it," she whispered and looked away from Sky.

Sky walked around the desk and positioned herself behind Snow's seated form. "Let me see your hand," she commanded.

Glistening eyes locked on Sky's and the women shared a poignant moment. Snow allowed Sky to lift her injured hand gently causing her leather armor to creak with the motion. Snow shifted her head first to the left and then to the right, each action resulting is a satisfying snap. "I feel drained," she whispered to Sky as her friend wiped away the blood from Snow's hand.

"No doubt," replied Sky.

Snow turned to look at her most trusted Sister, who busied herself wrapping Snow's hand in a delicate white cloth. The square covered the worst of the cut as the white embroidered apple absorbed Snow's blood. The white-on-white apple transformed before her eyes to a dark red.

Sky finished wrapping Snow's hand and took a step back. "Do we respond to this latest development?" she asked.

Snow shook her head, her dark curls bounced. "To respond would be to reveal that we have acquired one of the mirrored fragments of legend." Snow rose from her wooden chair. "I have many sisters, but only one daughter..." Snow's voice faded as emotion overcame her.

"I understand, my Queen," Sky said in solemn reverence.

"Ha! Queen." Snow heaped as much derision as she could on her title. "A queen usurped by her own husband under the control of an evil sorceress. A queen who hides in the mountains while her subjects bow and scrape to violent subjugation. Bowing to that..." Her voice raised, and she squeezed her eyes closed allowing the thought to perish lest it poison her soul.

Snow opened her eyes, ablaze with compassion and strength. They'd always been the eyes of a ruler, but Sky saw a new fire burn. A menacing fire. "Ready project Muted Sight," Snow commanded, her voice hardening. "I want him in the castle as soon as possible."

∼

CLICK.

The sound was as familiar to Ceridwen as her own breathing. She looked at her subjects to see if any of them had noticed the sound. As if the mindless Tenyks would notice, she thought and watched everyone go about their business.

Click.

Ceridwen shifted uncomfortably in her throne of brass. A puff of steam escaped from beneath her elegant gown. She held her hand out and studied the fine lines on her fingers. It's time, she thought and rose. The throne room was suddenly silent as all eyes turned to their ruler. Even in the silence, no one but Ceridwen was aware of the metal-on-metal shifting beneath her gown.

Click.

"Bring me one of the captured rebels!" she bellowed as she walked stiffly to her antechamber.

In her private room, she removed her gown and examined herself in a full-length mirror. Her gaze focused on her brass legs. The magic façade had faded, and the whirling gears refracted candlelight on the walls and ceiling. She adjusted her bosom and turned, so her profile was reflected in the mirror, sucking in her abdomen.

"Mirrored fragment, with sight so clear, tell me now if danger's near." A recess in one of her brass legs opened and she withdrew a mirrored fragment. She aimed the fragment toward the full-length mirror, and it reflected a peeled face from within the fragment. Shadows and highlights reflected off each other, the infinite manifestation forming a visage with blind eyes, but a sight known across the nine kingdoms.

The magic mirror fragment's reply was interrupted by a stern rap on her chamber door. Ceridwen sighed and replaced the fragment. She walked to her bed, sat on the edge, and covered her legs with a blanket before announcing, "Enter!"

A Tenyk ushered in a young man. The rebel's sightless waxen eyes darted around the room. Ceridwen smiled, as she watched the man's eyes move to and fro, a habit left over from when the centers of his eyes comprised a color other than white.

"The rebel, per your command, my queen," said the Tenyk, pushing the blind man forward.

Ceridwen looked from the rebel to her subject. His eyes had color, but they lacked the spark of life. The Tenyk was oblivious to the nakedness of his queen. Pity, she thought, as she examined the Tenyk. His broad shoulders and muscular chest rippled beneath the taut fabric straining to cling to his neck. "Leave him," she commanded. A smile the Tenyk could not see spread across her lips. "You will make yourself available to me this evening."

"As you wish, my queen," the Tenyk droned before he turned on his heel and closed the chamber doors behind him.

~

Tell mother I love her.

"Again."

Sky watched Reese die once again. She felt something heavy in her chest. John cradled Reese's body, and before the glass eye sailed out of view, Sky saw Rees's lips try to form her next words. She knew those lips. Even aged as they were, Reese's high cheekbones were the same young ones Sky caressed at night. She would know Reese's attempt to say her name no matter where or when her beloved was.

"Again."

The scene moved forward with precision. She imagined she heard the bones in Reese's chest crack as the chunk of rock struck her. It had only been a few weeks since Reese left on her mission to protect their "future" king. A king who willingly bit the poisoned apple, she thought as the life faded from Reese's eyes yet again.

"Again."

She traced her finger over Reese's lips as they spoke their last words. A teardrop distorted the image, and Sky closed her eyes, imagining the intimate moments with Reese, instead of the broken woman she saw in the fragment. The fierce warrior woman façade unraveled with each subsequent viewing.

"Again," she whispered.

*C*eridwen looked down on the broken form of the Tenyks. He had been nearly perfect once. *Once.* Except that there were some things that her brass legs just did not allow, no matter how strong the desire still burned. Her rage was slightly assuaged by the Tenyks harsh death by her bare hands.

She turned again to the rebel prisoner, knowing that what his eyes couldn't see, his mind visually improvised. She knew he had heard much, smelled much, and, she was certain from the splatter, felt much too. But the smell, *the smell was primal.* It tapped into depths of fear beyond vision. People who woke from vivid nightmares could tell themselves it was "just a dream." A mere figment of fancy conjured by the mind in the dark of the night. To wake in terror without vision *was* fear. Fear itself. Not an illusion of fear diluted by the staid limits of experience and imagination, but pure, harsh fear. "Blinding Fear'" may have been bandied about by generations of Old Wives, but they certainly didn't create it.

Ceridwen smiled at her internal monologue. She turned to the not-so-broken man, his shoulders squared in defiance, and said, "So now, my blind rebel, let us see what you know..."

SNOW SAT ON HER THRONE. AT FIRST GLANCE, IT LOOKED a pitiful mess of polished sticks wickered together in a rush. The more one studied it, though, the more complex, interwoven patterns emerged. Snow found it relaxing to lose herself in thought while mentally tracing its intricate lines. Today, though, it was all about business. She regretted that since, for all of its subtle beauty, the throne was startlingly uncomfortable. At least she never worried about ever looking less than fully alert while enthroned, let alone sleepy!

"They are here, my Queen," Sky announced gravely.

"Yes, yes we're here. Not like you'd mistake us for anyone else would you *Queenie?*" said the first of seven short men with long beards and round bellies. "Since we're the only damned dwarfs for a hundred leagues or more."

"Of course, King Odc. And, thank you for attending me."

"Attending *you?* We're not your subjects! These are *our* caves, whatever cockamamie title you call yourself!" raged a Dwarf clad all in red.

"Now, now, Prymgu, have you looked around? It's not like the humans have a lot of 'royalty' to choose from," laughed a dwarf all in silver.

"Manners Pypha! You've done insulted her!" said King Odc, shushing them to silence before turning back to Queen Snow. "Right. You called us. So. What do you want?"

"Very well, King Odc, I called upon you because I have considered your offer and I consent to your plan."

King Odc glared at the dwarfs again; Pypha had taken to burying his face in his arm and was unsuccessfully trying to hide his laughing behind the brown-clad Lubfash, who now found himself uncomfortably at the front of the dwarven contingent. With his men now, marginally, quiet, Odc addressed Snow, "As much as I, we, appreciate that Queenie, we weren't really asking permission."

"Nope. Nope. Nope," interrupted Poedy, who was wearing more patches than clothes, none of which matched.

Odc gave up glaring, "As *I* was saying, we are not your subjects Queen White. Much like we're letting you use our caves, for the time being, our talking to you about our plan was merely a polite courtesy. We started sapping the same night we spoke."

Snow said nothing for a moment but gripped the chair hard enough that some of the branches shook. She looked past the dwarves trying to calm herself before speaking. Slowly, ever so slowly, she regained control and was happy to see the dwarves had taken a step back from her throne.

"If *I* lose, Master Dwarf, we *all* lose. Yes, *all* of you. That's why I keep urging caution. And I'm sorry, but am I *boring* you!?" she shouted at a dwarf dressed all in blue yawning into his hands.

"Sorry Queen," Pelyse said, "long night sapping."

Finished with the encounter, Queen Snow stood. "Enough with you. Come with me now and brief my generals. They need to hear this immediately." They filed out of the throne room in a twisting line headed to the war room with Snow in the lead. The last dwarf hung back to inspect the throne's workmanship more carefully when he violently sneezed.

"Clean it up, Zesnye!" shouted King Odc without turning around.

~

"OH, YOU POOR, *POOR* THING, YOU'RE TREMBLING. HERE, let me help you take that wet shirt off," Ceridwen said to the speechless rebel. "It's ok, you don't need to speak." She bared her teeth and smiled, knowing that the rebel sensed it. "Yet," she concluded, as did her smile.

After a moment she grinned at him again while lifting the shirt over his head. Even though he couldn't *see* it, she knew he could *feel* it. *Primally.* "You can tell me what I want to know, my dear blind man, or..." She paused and allowed her eyes to roam over the man's bare chest. "Or," she continued, "you can please me." She gently ran her hand along his smooth face, pulling it closer to hers, to where he could smell the sweet traces of tea on her breath.

"Nothing to say, my blind rebel? Are you mute too?"

She smiled again as he shook his head "no."

She grasped his hand with a delicate touch and rubbed it across her face. "Do you like my skin? I'm sure you do," she added with a sulky chuckle before running his hand down her back and along her side, pausing before slowly bringing it up and moving his hand to cup her breast.

"Squeeze me, my blind man," she whispered, applying pressure on his hand. "Please me and I shall I release you."

She sighed as he squeezed again without her guidance. Then, inhaling deeply and taking his hand, she slowly moved it down her stomach to where her brass legs began. She laughed at his confusion, and then cackled at the horror on his face as she snapped her legs together, breaking his hand.

"Where there is no pleasure, rebel, there is only pain."

~

CERIDWEN RAN FROM HER CHAMBER SCREAMING FOR HER Tenyks. "Below! Below!" she shrieked. "There is a tunnel below the keep! Rally! Rally all! Head down at once and defend the Keep! Defend it to the last of you!"

Tenyks ran from her, scattering like leaves in a gust of wind. Some headed below the keep right away, while others issued orders to the groups they were charged with. Ceridwen felt a wash of fear creep over her. Her Tenyks' were at their weakest when relying on their own initiative, a situation unavoidable when fighting in the dark, unknown catacombs below her Oossah Keep.

She bit her knuckle in a mix of fright and fury, only to knock her tooth on its smooth, brass surface. She had lost complete control of the spell, and her true, metal form had almost consumed her again. Given the current threat, it wasn't worth the expenditure of magick to mask. She may well yet need the reserve from the men she'd already killed. *One and a half, really,* she thought, as her mind returned to its cold pragmatism. She needed a contingency plan for herself. With no reflections, she couldn't use the mirror's magick shard to guide the battle as she had before. Her only hope was that it wasn't too late, and the Tenyks could overwhelm Queen White's forces.

~

SNOW WHITE LOOKED OUT OVER THE RANKS OF HER Sisters. There were more of them than she had ever thought possible. Her elevated view from her steed and the slight rise in the cavern floor afforded her the authority that the Sisters' readily gave. Their uniforms were not just for quick identification in battle, but also to make determining their number that much harder for Ceridwen's spies. Mounted women with spears, sabers, and cutlasses patted and reassured their nervous steeds. There weren't enough horses for everyone to have, so those that did trained long and hard with their equine partners. All eyes turned to their warrior queen.

"My dearest Sisters," she said, choking up just a bit, "you have always filled me with such pride." She paused as an appreciative rumble cascaded over the gathered warriors. "Whether it was in the desperate hours of our flight from she who would usurp us, the carving of a new life for us below ground, or even-" she paused to gather her breath. "Or even when we did everything, *everything,* that had to be done to ensure our safety. You have stood tall against every challenge. And now, we have one last battle to fight."

This time, the vocalization from the Sisters was an eager growl, echoing louder off rough-hewn walls than only moments before. "We have been waiting for this moment a long time," Snow continued, "it has taken years of patience and fortitude to reach this point, to align ourselves so the blow we strike will be a killing one. Ceridwen's power is immense, but I shan't give her the honor of 'Queen' or 'Ruler' or any other title beyond, 'Criminal.' Today we march. We shall strike the final blow in our war against her, and our freedom shall finally be at hand!"

The gathered Sisters erupted in cheers, hollers, and other cries of exuberance. Snow smiled at their display of fanatical devotion to their cause and dismissed her desire to shush them, lest they alert Ceridwen to their presence.

"Ride my Sisters, ride! It is our past, our present, and our future that we shall now avenge! Ride!" Though her final exhortation was lost in the cacophony of hoof beats, footfalls, and clattering of armor.

~

KING JOHN REMOVED THE GOLDEN APPLE FROM THE scale, turning his back on the creaking door to the secret chamber. The glass shard in his other hand had gone blank after briefly clouding over like the morning mist. He paused and revised his previous thought: *more like the fetid mist rising from a putrid swamp.* He felt the weight of both, no longer surprised that the shard weighed more. He looked up to Heaven in supplication for strength and confirmation of his path.

The Gods, though, as ever, were silent to him as he slumped to his knees in despair.

~

SNOW WALKED DOWN THE SLIGHT RISE AFTER dismounting as the last of her Sisters marched out of the cavern. She had but two additional pieces of business to attend to before she could join them in glorious battle.

"Friend Dwarves," she said to the awkward seven figures before her, "my gratitude is upon you. If you wish to fight, I will not stop you. If you would like to stay, I will not implore you. You have already done your part better than I could have ever dreamed."

"We will do as we intended," replied King Odc with a scowl, "you do not rule over us."

Snow hid her smile at the unfortunate choice of words by the dwarven king. "I realize this, King Odc, I would merely offer an idea." She paused to size up the stout man. "A plan if you will."

"I knew it!" bellowed Prymgu, "I told you all! She's never going to be done! Well!? What would you have us do now?"

"Easy there," commanded the leader of the dwarves, taking the conversational reins again. "What is your 'thought' Queen White?"

Ever the strategist, Snow detailed her contingency plan should the worst befall the battle against Ceridwen and the Tenyks.

~

CERIDWEN WALKED DOWN CORRIDORS SUDDENLY QUIET AS the last of the Tenyks descended into the tunnels and catacombs below her purloined palace. Each step of her brass legs echoed that much more across desolate halls as she planned for, and against, the possibilities of the coming battle. Thoughts ran through her head; looking, seeking, for connection, but they struggled against the quietus of her solitude.

Her solitude... The Tenyks were all in the tunnels...

They were *all* in the tunnels, leaving *her* alone...

"It's a trap!" she screamed into the emptiness, her cry echoing off of pristine stonework. She lumbered toward her chambers, her magick forgotten, to prepare for what was to come.

*J*ohn placed the last rock over Reese's grave. The shallow scrapings were hardly befitting a proper burial of a woman so profound; he lacked the empathy to see. He didn't fully understand the concepts she bandied about, but he detected a love she harbored for him. It lived just below the surface – not a romantic love, but a familial love. *Who was Reese,* he thought, *and when does she come from?*

⁓

"PUSH, SNOW, PUSH!"

John saw the malice in his wife's eyes. Her façade of being the loving queen was nonexistent here with the midwife observing the joyous proceeding.

Snow closed her eyes and bore down as a scream escaped her lips. John was used to seeing the prim and proper Queen White, but the sweat that dripped from Snow's brow, and the pain that showed on her face, was a side of her he had fortunately never before seen.

The reserved passion she displayed in manners of state were hidden behind her ghostly pallor. If their child possessed a fraction of the intensity his wife had, then the kingdom was in good hands.

John's reverie was interrupted by a wail. His unfocused eyes scanned his queen, and their... *princess.*

"John," Snow whispered, "come hold your daughter."

John gently held the swaddled child. "My sweet baby of ardor," he announced to all in attendance.

Snow rolled her eyes and motioned for the infant to be returned to her. Her new child fussed, and Snow hoped the baby would relieve more discomfort soon.

"She's hungry," John declared. "Baby Reese and my glowing queen need some time alone."

As he handed Reese back to Snow, the room cleared. Clerics to witness the birth of their princess; historians to scratch on parchment, chronicling the event; and royal guards to oversee all the other people crowded into the small room. The midwife had insisted the room be free of any decorations or furniture other than a bed and a few wooden chairs. *Especially mirrors.*

"We are *not* naming her that!"

John looked over his shoulder at the retreating historians. "I think it may be too late. Besides, how else would we honor our ancestry?"

Snow scowled at her husband. "Fine," she said. "I'll name the next one."

John rushed to her side and held her free hand. "I decree it," he whispered, mischief in his eyes. "Shall I ask the historians to return, and make it official?"

Snow dropped her husband's hand and cradled their new baby. "I expect great things from baby Reese," she replied as the baby nuzzled her breast.

~

JOHN MADE HIS WAY DOWN THE MOUNTAIN, AND FROM THE grave of the mysterious woman, named Reese, who spent the last few years mentoring him. The pulverized boulder was less than a few hundred paces away, as were the gleaming metal remnants of a killing machine. It was mostly intact, but for the mangled left arm and missing head.

He stood there, staring at the monstrosity that attempted to kill him, and let out a slow breath.

"A marvel of workmanship," a voice intoned.

John whirled, and a stout man with a fiery red beard stood a few paces away. "Your name, good dwarf?" responded John.

"Odc is the name my kin have given me," the dwarf replied.

"Master Dwarf," John responded, "from what kin do you hail?"

Odc nodded as if he gleaned the unasked question. "We hail from beyond the seven mountains."

"I implore you, Odc, take this monstrosity and hide it well."

Odc looked to the brass automaton, and back to John. "This is quite the task for which you ask."

John returned Odc's steely gaze. "I offer payment of your choosing if I am able," he replied.

Odc's eyes fell to John's tattered clothing. "My payment is seven-fold," he responded. "A chair of plain wood to adorn my supper table."

John nodded.

"An earthenware plate to hold my supper."

John nodded again.

"A loaf of bread baked by your own hands."

John looked at his hands briefly before he nodded yet again.

"Vegetables cultivated and picked on this very mountain."

John stared at Odc, the stout man projecting a defiant stance that only dwarves seemed to master.

"I shall need a fork and knife of brass to eat my bread and vegetables."

John started to nod once more, but Odc continued: "A mug to hold my drink as I sup with my kin."

"We have an accord, Sir Odc," replied John, his hand extended. "I shall endeavor to get your payment post-haste."

Odc grasped his hand. "I do not wish these items right away."

"When?"

Odc winked and turned on his heel. "You will know when, Master Huntsman," he called over his shoulder as he disappeared into the thicket.

The words echoed in John's mind as he climbed down the mountain toward his home and the life of a huntsman.

~

"FATHER, WHY DO WE DO SET AN UNUSED PLACE every day?"

King John ruffled his daughter's hair. "To remind us of a promise I made so many years ago."

Reese looked from her father to her mother. Snow nodded and placed a linen cloth below the earthenware plate, brass knife, fork, and mug. A single wooden chair sat in front of the table. John had made it before he was tasked to kill Snow. He never told Snow the story behind the odd custom, but she recognized the items from her own adventure in the forest so many years ago.

Reese reached for the bread and vegetables, but a stern look from Snow stayed her hand. John placed the vegetables and bread on the plate at the empty space at their table.

The royal family ate their supper as they had for years. They were loved by their subjects and were not prone to extravagant meals and parties. As servants came to clear the table, and the uneaten portions, they knew the cold vegetables and bread would be dispersed to the orphans in the orphanage Snow spent so much time attending.

"Mi'Lord," an excited voice sounded from the corridor.

Snow and Reese excused themselves as the crier stood at attention beside John.

"At ease soldier," John commanded.

"Mi'Lord," the crier announced, "there is an old crone with urgent news of the Rookskye family."

～

"Who has eaten my bread?"

"Those are my vegetables, wench!"

Odc picked up his displaced brass mug. "Boys," he said to the rabble stomping around the room. When no one heeded his words, he bellowed, "Boys!"

His six companions looked to their leader. "The oracle has foretold this moment." Odc looked to the young woman peeking out from behind an immense wardrobe. "Come out, girl."

Seven pairs of eyes followed Snow as she stepped away from the wardrobe. She smoothed the front of her dress and curtseyed to the gathered faithful. The silence was palatable, and could've used a side dish. Unfortunately, Snow ate the hoarded bread and vegetables.

"Master dwarf," Snow knelt at Odc's feet.

"The Tenyks are advancing on us, Highness."

Snow blinked at the words that didn't belong. "Master dwarf?" she asked.

"Snow," an urgent voice penetrated her dream.

Snow woke with a start, and her grip tightened on the lance that lay across her lap.

"They're almost upon us," Sky hissed in her ear.

Snow peeked out from her hidden vantage, and the dream faded into the recesses of her memory. "Now!" shouted Sky as the roof of their hiding spot sprang open and the sisters followed.

Sky rebounded off the hatch, her twin brass scimitars brandished with the tips brushing her elegant elbows. Her strike with the pommel missed her first target, only to have the scimitar slash across the throat of the missed target as her fist hit home against the Tenyk beside. A fountain of blood erupted from the downed Tenyk, drenching the tips of Sky's blond hair strawberry.

Willow rose high enough for her clockwork crossbow to clear the blind. The twang of the brass line was a language only she knew. Recoiling, the stock reset and a brass cylinder rotated another bolt, knocked into position. Steam hissed from her matching brass forearm bracers as each bow loosed death into the advancing horde. She waded into the bodies, her braided hair swinging to and fro with each duck and weave.

Snow's gaze shifted. *Where is Daisy?* she thought, surveying the battlefield. An explosion of noise and steam flung the mindless Tenyks as Daisy's gauntleted hands swung a Tenyk by the ankles, his body bludgeoning all obstacles in her path. When her brilliant gauntlets were dripping in Tenyk blood, and her weapon was pulverized into a boneless lump, she discarded it and seized another of the horde. Daisy's close-cropped red hair didn't show the blood of her enemies, but her white teeth brandished through a mask of blood and gore formed a smile as she spat globs of viscera over her shoulder.

Snow watched as Sky's blade erupted from the chest of a hapless Tenyk, her knee striking the body to slide it from her weapon. Sky met Snow's eyes, and they exchanged a look and a wink. Snow spun her lance, wedged the handle into a crevasse and vaulted into the fray. She ran the bladed edge through three Tenyks, before she twisted the handle, and steam forced the shaft to collapse on itself. Another twist and the lance snapped to its original position. Again, she planted the handle, and once more she leaped into a group of Tenyks pushed back by Daisy's unstoppable fury.

The quartet dispatched the Tenyks, using the walls and ceilings of the tunnel to outmaneuver the pitiful, mindless men. Each death Snow witnessed weighed on her heart. These men and boys she once called her subjects, had had their souls stolen by an evil that knew neither bounds nor limitations. Ceridwen was a blight on the world, and she moved from kingdom to kingdom consuming everything in her quest for something as arbitrary as *beauty.*

Even with all her dark magick, Ceridwen couldn't match the beauty of a young Snow White. What did her envy get her? A broken magic mirror, and a body of brass. Snow was certain Ceridwen was now more machine than human as her unattainable quest for perfection and beauty consumed her twisted mind.

Snow stood over the fallen Tenyks, valuable tears etching gullies into the dirt and blood that caked her face. Her three Sisters didn't echo her sadness. To them, the Tenyks were an enemy army to be defeated. To Snow, they were brothers, uncles, and children. Sky, Willow, and Daisy congratulated each other and slapped each other on the shoulders and backs. None of them would know the sorrow of killing her own people.

~

CERIDWEN BOUNDED INTO THE THRONE ROOM antechamber. "Where is it?" she asked of an elegiac King John.

John looked up and sneered, the mirrored fragment that had ruled him for so long clouded over. "I'll never help you!" he shouted. "Your hold over me is finished!"

Ceridwen kicked him in the stomach, and picked him up by his throat, the clockwork and steam forcing her artificial limbs to her command. John beat his fists against her magnificent gleaming arm as his vision faded. "You have failed," he whispered as the light in his eyes faded.

Ceridwen screamed and tossed John's body against the throne. She didn't even listen for the telltale sound of broken bones. Turning toward the false wall, she cocked her arm and let loose a brass fist against the stonework. Each impact smashed brick and dented her fingers a little more. Her fingers would need replacing, but she was almost through the stone barrier.

As the hole widened enough to grant her ingress, Ceridwen saw her creation stomping up the stairs. She stood aside as pressure built up, and the brass automaton crushed the stone that remained between them.

The Automaton seized Ceridwen by her metal waist and leaped through the roof of the throne room. She saw Jarvis limp up the steps and prostrate himself at the site that the mechanical beast had vacated. Ceridwen cocked her head slightly, and the Automaton set her down before dropping back into the throne room to retrieve a grateful Jarvis. A leap back to the roof and her creation held them both in its arms and thundered into the sky.

Ceridwen looked back as Snow and her warrior Sisters clamored into the throne room. They could only watch helplessly as the greatest menace their kingdom had ever seen disappeared into a pristine cloudless, azure sky.

Snow tore her eyes from the limp form of her husband. Willow and Daisy covered the man with a tapestry wretched from the throne room's wall by falling debris. Snow tapped one end of a discarded clouded mirror shard against her cheek as she contemplated the battle for Oossah Keep. After a stern salute and hasty retreat, Snow was left only with her closest confidant.

"My Queen?" Sky stammered, as she turned back from Willow and Daisy's trotting departure.

"Yes, Sky?" Snow answered, facing her Sister with a forced smile. "You wonder at my mood?"

Sky's eyes narrowed, and she played absently with her dirty hair. "Yes," she replied.

"I smile because what was lost in battle may yet win us the war."

"I don't understand, your Majesty. We were late, and that brass man saved Ceridwen the death she's earned."

"Brass, yes. Not a man, though, but a woman."

"A woman? Are you sure?"

"Yes, a Man's body, to be sure, but a woman none the less. It is her heart, her very blood, that powers the clockwork shell." Snow stepped away from Sky with the clouded shard toward the far window. Rubble from the roof littered the room, as did the bodies of those that had fallen. She felt grief at men and Tenyks alike, for what was a Tenyks but a man whose free will Ceridwen stole? For her Sisters, though, for them, the hurt was a wave of cold emptiness trying to drown her. She knew them all. *Sisters* more than in name, but in the eternal bond of love and honor.

She knew all of them by sight, even when the bodies were no longer whole. She walked around the room in its entirety, taking a circular, zig-zagging path to the window. For each of her Sisters, she thought of their name as their memory flooded her mind. Often smiling, sometimes merely profound; each image flashed was a defining moment between the Sister and their queen.

At the window, she summoned Sky over to help her take off her breastplate. As the two undid the leather straps binding front and back together, Snow felt the first, slow trickle of a tear down her cheek. "Please," she said, quietly imploring Sky, "Help me lift this over my head before I lose another." Sky raised the armor over Snow's head, setting it below the ledge.

Free of the armor, Snow retrieved an opaque bottle secured between her breasts by a simple silk cord around her neck. She looked outside at the bleak, desolation of the land, *her* land, surrounding the keep, and another knife of inconsolable grief stabbed through her gut. She sunk to her knees in the shattered remains of the throne room and let herself cry without restraint.

Through blurred eyes she undid the bottle's stopper and collected as many of her tears as she could, hating herself for having to harvest her own sorrow. Finally, mercifully, the tears and her shudders ebbed into quiet pain. She looked up at Sky's red eyes.

"This is the first I've known you to cry, Sky," she said, reaching out a hand to her dearest Sister.

"It's just the dust in the room from the roof collapse, I'm sure," Sky replied, letting go of Snow's hand. Though not without a quick squeeze first.

Snow stood again, taking her Sister by the shoulders and staring her in the eye. "I need you to take this bottle and this shard to the edge of Rennoc Woods. You will find King Odc there, and you are to give him both. Whatever he may then ask of you, however wrong it may feel, you need to do it." She paused and fought back another surge of emotion. "For me," she concluded.

"But, my Queen? I don't know-"

"Yes, dear Sky, you do. You are the only one I trust. I think I know what King Odc will need you to do, but I imagine it will feel like something beyond your ability. I ask you to trust that I know more of this than I can share. And, that King Odc knows even more than I."

"Remember, Sky, Dwarves were birthed by magick itself to keep balance in this world. There are things they can do, things they can see, things they can *know;* that we cannot."

"I understand Your Highness. But I have never left your side before. Not when there was still a fight to be had."

"And I think, Sky, that you will soon enough be at my side again," Snow answered with a small smile. "Will you promise me you will do this? I do not trust any other Sister as I do you, nor is there any other Sister as capable."

"I will your Majesty," Sky answered, taking a knee and solemnly bowing before Snow.

"I am no longer 'Your Majesty' to you, Sky, but simply 'Snow.'"

Sky left Snow's side trying to hide her sudden grin. She paused at the hole in the roof, a ragged sunbeam illuminating her as she stopped and looked up. She turned back to Snow, hesitating with a decision. "Your Majesty ... *Snow*," she interjected deliberately, as though tasting the word in her mouth as she spoke it, "how do you know that the," she spat the words, "brass automaton had the heart of a woman. I saw it not."

"Magick touches time differently," Snow answered. "It is not easily understood, but think of yourself. Now you cannot only call me by name freely, but I encourage you to do so. Before, mere minutes ago, to do such a thing would be unthinkable to you! Yet, both of these Skys are the same, even as they are different. The same woman separated only by time. To magick, they exist together, even as time demands their distinction."

"But-" Sky started as a confused scowl marred her lovely features.

Snow smiled and squeezed Sky's shoulder. "Her magick has, and shall, become so dark it mocks the prohibitions of time itself, Sky, letting the past, present, and future brass automatons exist simultaneously. Ceridwen's brass legs betrayed her as being the one, and *only*, brass automaton. It was Ceridwen's sad past that saved her present horror."

~

SKY WALKED ALONG THE EDGE OF RENNOC WOODS TAKING grim solace in Cloud Dancer's ease. The roan gelding wasn't even so much as wicking despite the unnatural quiet. On the outskirts of the Wilds, this area was too far from anything to have been more than lightly touched by Ceridwen's Evil. She was following the long, undulating tree line with her eyes when she felt Cloud Dancer pull back on his lead. She casually continued on for a few steps before dropping his lead, spinning and drawing her brass scimitars.

"Good morning, Mistress Sky," King Odc said, holding out a hand of oats to Cloud Dancer. She gave Cloud Dancer only the briefest of glares with a near silent mutter of, "Traitor," before sheathing her scimitars and regarding the stout king of the dwarfs.

"And a good morning to you too, your Highness. I have been dispatched by-"

"The Queen, yes, we know," snapped Prymgu, emerging from the underbrush with the rest of the dwarves, "That is *why* we're here, surrounded by trees and grass instead of decent rock."

"I *am* impressed. I've never let anyone sneak up on me, let alone seven," Sky said with a grudging nod toward the Dwarf King.

"That's because they weren't dwarfs," sneered Prymgu, just as Poedy tripped in the underbrush with a loud crash, tumbling and rolling down the slight embankment to a stop at Sky's feet.

"You were saying Master Prymgu?" Sky said as Poedy looked up at her with a resigned grin.

Instead of answering, Prymgu merely stalked off beyond the placid Cloud Dancer to stare with unkempt hostility at the distance in silence beside Lubfash.

With a small shake of her head for Prymgu, Sky knelt

before Odc, and a leather pouch from inside her cloak. He undid its bindings pulling out the shard and stoppered bottle. He undid the stopper and gently wafted its essence towards his prodigious nose before dropping to his knees next to Sky. "Is this..." he paused, re-stoppering it as the other six encircled the kneeling pair. "Are these Queen White's tears?"

"Yes, Her Majesty wept over her fallen Sisters, though in truth, I believe her heart grieves for every loss that Ceridwen has caused, be it Sister, Tenyks, horse, or tree."

They murmured variations of, "powerful magick," among themselves as Sky looked up in wonderment. "I don't understand, King Odc. Even when Snow tried to explain it to me, it still made little sense."

"Some spend a lifetime studying magick, and it still makes naught sense for them either. Time keeps everything from jumbling together all at once, but magick isn't so persnickety. A clouded shard and this vial of tears can only mean your queen is after the Enchanted Mirror itself."

"But this shard came from the Enchanted Mirror when it was destroyed." Sky paused to recall the tale. "A brass goblet thrown at the most inopportune time."

"Aye," King Odc replied with a nod. "Meaning that Queen White wants to destroy it thoroughly this time." He smiled and continued, "Through all of time."

"She wants to destroy a mirror that was already destroyed?" Sky asked, the sarcasm dripping from her voice.

"Essentially yes!" Zeysne said with more excitement than Sky could ever remember from him, as he punctuated his statement with a sneeze.

"Zeysne knows more magick lore than the rest of us combined," vouched King Odc with a solemn nod.

"You see," started Zeysne, stifling another sneeze, "The unbroken mirror and shard exist outside of time's domain through magick."

"How does that not lead to chaos?" asked Sky. "How is that *not* chaos?"

"We think, *think,* that since both time and magick ultimately lead to chaos, they cannot be wholly unalike. The only real difference is that time's rules are straightforward and strict, while magick's are arcane and malleable. What your queen has given us is the means to use magick's rule that 'like' things interact with greater strength to find the Enchanted Mirror.

"This shard was sundered from the mirror when it, 'died.' These tears, already potent magick themselves, also came from deep loss." Zeysne paused to sneeze before continuing, "So we can use the tears to reanimate the shard, loss for loss. The connection will be so strong, it'll create a line to the Enchanted Mirror visible enough for us to follow, if only for a short time."

Sky gasped. "You can actually *see* magick?"

"Me?" Zeysne shook his head. "No, unfortunately, though it would immensely help my studies. No, the only one of us who can actually see the ripples of magick is Pelyse."

"Yeah," interjected Prymgu, "because he's always half in that world anyway!"

King Odc saw Sky's frustration and took her hand. "The world of dreams is the veil between our world of time and the world of magick. Zeysne will use the queen's tears of sorrow to renew the shard, creating a connection to the Enchanted Mirror that Pelyse can see, thus letting us track it to where Ceridwen hid it."

Sky yanked her hand from King Odc's grasp. "And then?" she demanded.

"*And then* we have a chance to not just end Ceridwen herself, but the very curse of her existence!"

Sky stood up with Odc, but her triumphant smile suddenly chilled at Odc's countenance.

"You, Sky, are going to have to help us, though, and it will be harder than anything you've ever done," he said gravely.

"Name it," she said, hearkening back to her talk with Snow.

"You must understand, it is the only way we will be able to undo the spell in its entirety."

"She told me you would ask something of me King Odc. I gave her my word. So name your task. I am ready."

"I know you believe you are, but this will require more commitment and discipline than you can imagine."

Sky inhaled deeply, remembering her promise, "I have prepared myself, King Odc-"

Prymgu interrupted her with a loud snort, "Bah! Enough! He just doesn't want to tell you you're going to have to kill your queen."

"*I* cannot..."

A guard rushed to the barred wall and examined the scene within.

"Please..."

Ceridwen writhed on the dusty floor, her hands clawing at her throat. Her gasps for breath and help were not lost on the guard, but he had been warned that the old crone was not to be trifled with.

"Help..."

Her bulging eyes and blue lips convinced the guard that she was not faking her injury. He withdrew a brass key and placed it slowly into the receptacle. When the door opened, Ceridwen gasped her last and lay still at his feet. He withdrew his cutlass and prodded her limp form. When he received no reaction, he lifted her frail body gently with his arms and supported her head with his shoulder.

Her woozy eyes opened slowly, and she spoke, "Save me," she coughed.

The guard's eyes widened with the realization that when the crone spoke, her lips made no movement. He laid her on the bed, and his fingers probed her withered jaw. His fingertips found purchase, but his eyes couldn't reconcile the difference that his fingers felt.

"Magick..." he whispered, and took a step back, thoughtless to the potential danger.

He watched her chest rise and fall in ragged breaths. He only considered his actions for a moment, before procuring a talisman hidden in the folds of his tunic. He held it aloft and passed the chained crystal over the sleeping Ceridwen. The magick aura waned as the crystal showed the guard her true form.

Arms transformed from liver-spotted to milky white. Wrinkled skin subsumed into supple, youthful flesh. Hair, a tangle of gray, hid luscious black curls.

The crystal hovered, and seemed to be repulsed by her sagging mouth. He stepped forward and forced the crystal to her lips. The crystal cracked, and the magick aura broke with it. He was left to stare down at a beautiful young woman. Her skin was as white as snow, her hair as black as ebony. Her lips...

The guard frowned at the brass mask covering her from chin to forehead. He wondered what beauty or horror the mask covered. *Surely,* he thought, *surely the beauty contained within matches the excellent example of femininity.*

Her breathing problem was evident: the brass formed nose was pinched, and the jaw was askew. It appeared as if the woman had fallen, and the impact had crushed part of the mask. The ragged breath he heard from her was from air rushing between malformed brass.

He gently lifted her head to search for what machinations hid her real beauty. A brass clasp secured the mask to her head, and a single brass link closed the clasp. The guard didn't need his cracked crystal to discern the magic emanating from the lowly link. He slid his cutlass betwixt the clasps and pried with all his strength.

The moon had moved out of view from the only window, and the apple orchard below returned to shadow by the time he had worked the brass back and forth enough to where it finally it separated from the mask. He lifted the mask from her head, and he couldn't help but stare at her lips. *Lips as red as blood.*

∼

A GONG SOUNDED FROM THE CASTLE. TORCHES ALONG the grounds multiplied as more guards were roused to join in the search. Tobias clutched the unconscious form to his chest and looked back at the earthworks separating the keep from the expansive apple orchard. He breathed deep to catch his breath. Although the young woman was petite, she was heavy to a man who spent his nights prowling the prison, and his days attempting peaceful slumber. No matter the attempt, something always awoke him, and he often performed his rounds in a slight daze of exhaustion. He would never complain, for the position and trust as a night guard was much coveted by his contemporaries. A job he knew he could now never return to.

He determined he had rested long enough, and stole a furtive glance back to the keep. He hefted the young woman who he refused to continue calling Ceridwen over his shoulder and jogged through the orchard, his destination the black mountains of Rooskye, across the Allooashinn River. He did not fear leaving Oossah soil, as his tale of treachery by the king and the incarcerated woman was all the proof he needed to prove his worth.

~

TOBIAS LEANED AGAINST AN OUTCROPPING OF ROCK. THE apple orchard was over the horizon, and the sound of the Allooashinn River was detectable among the sounds of the forest.

A sharp noise sounded from the dense thicket. *A sneeze,* he determined, while drawing his cutlass. He had barely the strength to wield it, but he reasoned that no one would be the wiser.

"Zesnye may as well be a member of the *Sneeze Guard.*"

Tobias watched as seven dwarfs materialized from the thicket. One of them ran his arm under his nose and scowled at the dwarf that had spoken.

"I am Master Odc, and I present to you the Dwarven Guard."

Tobias looked from dwarf to dwarf, not lowering his cutlass. "I seek safe passage for me and my companion to the black mountains of Rookskye."

Odc nodded and looked at the still form at Tobias's feet. He turned to a dwarf dressed all in blue. "Is it her, Pelyse?"

Pelyse nodded slowly, leaned against a tree, closed is eyes, and snored softly, his blue coif covering his eyes.

Odc regarded Tobias. "We will grant *her* safe passage, but what about you, keep guard?"

Tobias lowered his cutlass.

An uptight dwarf clad in all red stepped forward. His

one-eyed stare seemed to sap what strength was left from an exhausted Tobias. "We should dispatch this meddlesome interloper." He emphasized his suggestion by swinging a large rock on the end of a brass handle over his head.

Odc replied, "No, no, Prymgu. We must follow the prophecy to the letter."

"A shame," Prymgu replied, looking at Tobias over his long, bulbous nose.

Odc turned toward the thicket. The Dwarven Guard moved to follow him. As the seven of them disappeared, Odc returned and glared at Tobias. "Well? Are you coming?"

Tobias glanced briefly at the rocks above that formed the black mountain. He sheathed his cutlass, hefted the sleeping woman, and followed the dwarves into the thicket, and the rocks below.

~

TOBIAS PUSHED HIS THREE-WHEELED WOODEN CART ALONG the uneven floor of the cavern the motley crew passed through. He was grateful for the expansive void and relatively smooth ground. The Dwarven Guard had to stop repeatedly to allow Tobias to rest, as the woman he rescued failed to regain consciousness. Odc examined her with his pair of spectacles before announcing she was in a cursed sleep, and even Zesnye's vast knowledge of the occult was not enough to break the spell.

Eventually, the dwarf without a beard discovered the wooden cart by stumbling against a rock wall which he fell through. The canvas covering the entrance to a maintenance room dropped, covering the group in dirt and other particulates.

Zesnye sneezed, as was expected; Prymgu scowled at the beardless dwarf; Pypha laughed heartily and shook the grime from his brown tunic like a wet dog sheds water. He finished the display by slapping his blue trousers clean, a chuckle accompanying each movement.

Although Lubfash was soft-spoken and apparently preferred to work alone, his prowess with tools was made evident by his disassembling several damaged carts to create one usable one. His brown outfit disguised the grease, but his green coif revealed the streaks of grime and oil. Tobias was impressed by the shy dwarf's mechanical skills.

Once the woman was secured in the cart, their journey continued, but now instead of stopping for Tobias to rest, they waited patiently as Tobias muscled the cart over obstacles.

～

ON THE THIRD DAY OF THEIR JOURNEY, PELYSE AWOKE with a shout that would've made Prymgu proud. "Danger, Odc!"

Odc rolled off his rucksack, and looked to Prymgu, who was already up, wielding his hammer, one eye closed, peering into the darkness beyond their fire that had burnt down to cinders.

"Stay your weapons, Dwarven Guard," a voice echoed off the stone walls.

"King John," whispered Pelyse.

"Show yourself, John," declared Odc.

A stately man appeared from the enveloping darkness. His frock coat and black trousers were barely distinguishable in the dim light. His waistcoat was a brilliant pinstriped purple, and instead of a silk puff tie, he wore a pair of goggles over his white collar. If his collar wasn't detached as it caught on his goggles, or his boots scuffed, betraying the oil used to maintain its color, he would've appeared regal.

"Give her to me," John declared, and looked past Tobias at the sleeping woman in the cart.

"You just wait a-" Tobias started but was interrupted by Odc.

"Our magick is but equal beneath the black mountain, King John." Odc heaped as much scorn on the honorific as he could.

"That may be true," replied John, "but I believe I have an advantage in *this* situation."

Odc squinted, and crossed his arms over his chest. "Do tell, *Your Majesty.*"

John rotated a Homburg in his hands and swatted at an unseen blemish. "Boots and blood," he replied nonchalantly as if Odc hadn't challenged him. The group became aware of soldiers suddenly as if a spell of seclusion had suddenly dropped.

Each soldier wore trousers, a jacket, and a rucksack. Brass helms covered their heads, and purple neckerchiefs hid their eyes.

"Now!" shouted Odc, and Zeysne threw a canvas pouch into the embers of their fire. A wave of *nothing* radiated in concentric circles from the flaming bag. John's eyes were focused on the fire, and his mouth hung agape, but, like his soldiers, he was frozen in time.

walking away from him was a figure in a dark cloak holding out a dim lantern for light.

"Halt!" John shouted, and the figure stopped.

John walked toward it when the figure held up an arm to its shrouded face beckoning silence before it motioned for John to follow and continued on its previous path. John wasn't sure why he didn't just call for the guards, choosing instead to quietly follow the figure. John lost sight of it as it turned the corner of the rampart heading toward the Orchard Gate. When John turned the corner himself he found the guards fast asleep, and the portcullis up. He was trying to rouse them when he looked up to see the figure standing halfway between the keep and the apple orchard. Even with the lamp held high, John could not make out the figure's face. John drew one of the guards swords and began trotting after the figure alert for whatever magick was afoot.

The figure turned and was quickly lost among the craggy shadows of the apple trees. John knelt beside the first row of trees, breathed as quietly as he could, and waited for a sign of movement. A twig snapped to his right, and he was off. Movement flashed again, and he turned to intercept the form. Ducking under a branch and dodging saplings, John burst into a hidden clearing within the orchard. With his eyes, now adjusted to the dark; and a gibbous Moon shining through a clear sky, John could see the clearing was really just a toppled tree giving way to the night.

From behind the fallen tree's gnarled trunk, the figure rose and held its lantern aloft. John readied himself, raised his sword and demanded, "Who are you? Show yourself!"

The figure's left hand raised and opened to reveal it was empty before slowly pulling its hood back and shaking loose long, blonde hair. John peered past the light of the lantern to see...

Reese!

John slumped to the ground in shock. Not his little Reese, his beloved daughter, but her namesake stood before him as surely as the ground beneath him was solid. He dropped the sword and rushed toward her, only to stop at her outstretched hand beckoning him to hold.

"Reese! How can this be?"

"I am, and am not Reese," she said in a cryptic whisper. "There have been many Reese's each in her own time, one whom you knew, loved, and watched die. I am another Reese, another facet of her whole, compelled here by the strength of her love for you."

"I do not understand," he said plaintively as if it was once again his own Reese as they were so many years ago, with her tutoring him through his confusion.

"You need not *understand.* You need only *act.* You must *trust* me, John."

"I *do* trust you, Reese," John declared, his eyes wet with unabashed tears.

"Do you remember the brass automaton? Our flight? Do you remember how I *knew* things? Things that were impossible to know?"

"They still haunt me," John whispered. "I trust you as I have no other, except my queen, Snow White."

"That's why I've come, John. A fortnight from now, Snow White, your queen will betray you."

~

JOHN RECOILED FROM THE FIGURE'S WORDS. FURY SURGED through him for even *considering* that this could be his Reese, his long dead tutor, compatriot, and *friend.* He scrambled back from the figure and seized his sword again as a glint of moonlight showed where he had dropped it.

"Foul creature! I shall have your blood!"

"I am Reese, John. You *loved* me. I am here through that love. Do you not remember us?"

"I will see you for what you are yet!" John exclaimed, holding the sword out and pulling a large, intricately cut Crystal on a thin, black cord from under his shirt. It was like the crystals issued to the Keep Guards for dispelling simple magicks, only this one was far, *far* more powerful. "We will see who you are, or *what* you are, soon enough."

He yanked on the cord to snap it free, and held the crystal aloft, its facets reflecting dots of moonlight around the dark clearing. He began slowly circling it above his head, waiting for the vapors of magick to vanish to see reality. As he waited for the Crystal to dispel the magick he found himself again indebted to the counsel of Jarvis for urging him to *always* wear the crystal. The crystal's pendulum turn smoothed its rhythmic thrumming - the only sound in the clearing. "Reese" merely stood there, hands folded and head cocked, looking at John with the patient disappointment he so well remembered from his most embarrassing of failures.

"How much longer are you going to need to see that I *am* Reese, John?"

"This can only be magick! Even if what you say is true, only magick can bring you to me."

"No, John, *love* brought me here. The love you shared with Reese was strong enough that the third power that binds reality together, *love,* summoned me."

"Magick and time are the only powers," he declared, remembering his lessons. Lessons that Reese herself had taught him.

"Magick and time are the only powers that *humanity* can control. That doesn't mean there isn't a third that is *not* controllable. Time is incessant with clear rules but without form. Magick can be shaped, but it waxes and wanes and is governed by capricious rules. *Love,* though," Reese smiled and stepped toward him, "love is stronger than either, but cannot be controlled by conscious thought or action. Since love does what love will, and can never be used otherwise, humanity always overlooks it."

"How do you know this then?" asked John, allowing the crystal to stop its perambulations.

"Because I am here. Because I am not the Reese you *knew* but *another,* that is *yet* her, and my heart can still *feel* her love for you. And, because my head knows the betrayal of Snow White, your queen. Only so high of a betrayal by one you so thoroughly love could have brought me here. Only another that *you* loved, and lost, could love beckon."

"Then speak," John commanded. He raised himself to

his full height and lowered his sword before continuing, "Speak of this betrayal you know."

"It gives me no pleasure to tell you this," Reese whispered, wiping tears from her delicate features. "Only I can know the depths of your love, and that you have given yet more to Snow White. It is because-"

"Hold, Reese, hold. I beg you, hold. I need not hear of love any longer." He stepped forward and grasped Reese by her shoulders. "Please just tell me of Snow's plans this coming fortnight."

Reese, again on the verge of tears, nodded her head in acknowledgment of John's request. "You have become a better man than I could have ever hoped," she said before she began to describe Snow's plans.

John became more ill with every revelation that passed Reese's lips.

∼

"THE SUN WILL NOT ALLOW ME TO STAY, JOHN," REESE said after she finished her long elocution.

John's sword remained embedded in the trunk, stabbed into it during the strongest wave of anger he had felt at Reese's words. Now, with that moment gone, and the full horror finally spoken, the two sat on the trunk with the sword between them. John let the words linger a bit longer before he spoke, "I'm sorry, Reese, I should have known you couldn't stay with me forever. I was just..."

She smiled and nodded. "Caught up in other things, yes. I understand. I really do. Please, just do me the favor of leaving me now. I know that I must surrender to the dawn, and I would have our parting be of *our* choice this time."

"Of course. It is the least I can do," he said and stood. He grasped his long-lost tutor's hands and whispered, "Thank you."

"You're welcome," she replied with a sheepish smile and stood as well.

He briefly tried wrenching the sword from the gnarled trunk before giving up when he saw how deep he had buried its blade. "It's just as well," he declared, letting go of its handle.

"Fare thee well, John."

"Farewell Reese," he replied, and turned rapidly to avoid her seeing the tears that had so quickly started streaming down his cheeks.

~

JOHN WALKED OUT OF THE CLEARING AND DISAPPEARED into the orchard without another glance back. He didn't hear Reese's sigh of relief.

She looked to her right at the sunlight just over the jagged peaks of the Broken Mountains. The timing had been closer than she had anticipated. If he hadn't *finally* noticed her walking by the kitchen door for the *seventh* time...

She slumped again on the trunk as the first of the Sun's rays lit her face, instantly washing away the magick and revealing true reality. He looked at his reflection in the sword's polished surface and chuckled as he imagined John's reaction to his beloved "Reese" instantly growing a beard and morphing into his "most trusted" advisor, Jarvis. He then downright laughed remembering the crystal.

"Oh John!" he said to a brightly ripened apple at his feet, "when will you ever remember that crystals can never dispel the magick of their creator?"

*R*eese's eyes snapped open at daybreak, and she disentangled herself from her bedfellow. She silently dressed in her cloth uniform, and her hand caressed the leather armor draped over the back of a chair.

"Sneaking off?" a voice called from the bed.

Reese spun and took in the view. Sky walked toward her slowly, and her hands fussed with her curly blonde hair. With Reese's help, Sky had washed the blood from her hair. After their night together, Sky stood unashamed of her nakedness. A flush rose on Reese's cheeks, and Sky smiled at the younger woman's embarrassment.

"As often as we bed, I would think you would be familiar with my body." Sky winked and retrieved her uniform from the floor.

A sharp knock on the door interrupted Reese's response. "Enter!" Sky shouted, and she continued to dress.

"Mi'Lady," a runner spoke, his blind eyes failing to discern the potentially embarrassing scene before him. "The chamber has been located."

Sky smiled. "Tell the elder sisters I will be there shortly."

The runner nodded and turned to leave. Reese let out

the breath she had held. "Sky..." she began, but Sky held up a finger to silence her.

"Speak not of it, Reese."

"But, mother..."

"Your mother is not just your mother!" Sky shouted before regaining her composure. "The queen has too much to worry about," she finished her sentence with a whisper.

Reese couldn't meet Sky's eyes, and they suited up in silence.

"Snow will be in the chamber," Sky declared, ad grasped Reese by the shoulders. "We can talk to her then if that is what you want."

Reese nodded and followed her commander out the door, sure of the events to come.

～

REESE WALKED A RESPECTFUL DISTANCE BEHIND SKY AS they entered the discovered chamber. Willow and Daisy nodded to Sky as she passed, ignoring Reese. It was only after Snow looked past them and saw Reese, that the women acknowledged the princess of a kingdom without a king or castle.

Snow smiled at her daughter and returned her attention to her most-trusted Sisters. She motioned for them to follow her through a shattered wall as the quartet stepped over debris. When Reese stepped into the breach, she saw it.

Hues of red snaked out as tendrils struck anything made of brass. Focusing on the center of dark magick was difficult. The colors shifted as ribbons unfurled and disappeared. It was the most beautiful thing Reese had ever seen, and that was saying much considering her present company.

The women studied the swirling vortex of unbidden magick unbound by time. They whispered in hushed tones and gesticulated wildly. Reese couldn't hear the conversation, but she knew each of the women, and it was likely that Sky, Willow, and Daisy wanted to use the portal to attack Ceridwen through time. The only surviving member of the Council of Nine would be the dissenting opinion. The imbalance of ideas was unimportant since Snow White was still their queen.

Daisy and Willow threw up their hands and walked away as Snow nodded to Sky. Sky produced a brass sphere, red tendrils from the portal licked its polished surface. Sky threw the sphere into the vortex, and as it pierced the event horizon, it floated, its machinations transforming the sphere. Steam hissed as the construct grew larger. All eyes were on the portal, so no one felt the shudder or the small shower of dust that rained down from the ceiling on all in attendance.

When the roof collapsed, only Reese had the presence of mind to draw her weapon. A brass hand reached out from the cloud of debris and dust seizing Reese's brass sword. The strength of the hand not only wretched the sword from her hand, but malformed the metal. A second arm appeared and shoved Reese back toward the swirling vortex and the construct that seemed to grow as it drank the dark magick.

"Reese!" Sky and Snow screamed at the same time. The brass man strode confidently toward the vortices and Reese.

Reese picked up a chunk of earthen wall and hurled it at the ambling behemoth. It batted away the piece with ease and continued its advance on the time portal. Reese found herself trapped between the machine and felt the touch of magick fingers on her back. She could hear her mother and sisters shouting over the din of the brass automaton and the noise from the collapsing portal.

The monstrosity reached with its brass fingers and seized the expanding brass construct. Reese worried that the automaton would somehow use the construct to absorb more magick, or prevent the destruction of the portal, and without forethought, she grasped the brass arm with all her might.

She instantly felt the magick throughout her being. She saw the chamber from an unnatural view. Sky was screaming, and her brass blade was lodged in the back of the metal man. A red glow surrounded her body, the automaton, and Sky. Reese heard and felt a timeless scream, not from herself, or Sky, but from the automaton.

∽

DAISY LURCHED FOR SKY'S SCIMITAR, but SNOW PUSHED her back and pointed at Daisy's brass gauntlets. Snow retrieved a sizable rock and brought it down on the glowing scimitar. The rock glanced off it, failing to free Sky from magick's embrace.

Snow felt rubble strike her back, and she scrambled out of the way as Daisy's brass gauntlets tore out a section of stone wall, and brought it down like a stone scythe, separating Sky from her scimitar at the wrist.

Freed from the magick, Sky collapsed to the floor, blood ebbed from her crushed wrist. Daisy looked to her Sister, and after a pecuniary nod from Sky, she closed her gauntleted fingers on Sky's wrist, twisting a collar on the gauntlet, causing it to glow with heat, searing Sky's injury to staunch the blood. The purchase of Sky's freedom complete. As Sky's vision faded, she saw tendrils of time tear apart her bedfellow ... and in a poof, Reese was gone. They then started on the brass automaton. As she lost consciousness, she knew Reese and the monstrosity were lost to the emptiness of time.

$\sim$

PISTONS MOVED, EACH THRUST ACCOMPANIED BY A PULSE of steam. The constant chuff-chuff and the sound of metal against metal were felt as well as heard. The unending vibrations radiated from ahead, as the locomotive behemoth dragged metal, glass, and leather along lines predetermined many years ago by engineers long since retired. Heat from flame barely contained boiled water, and that water generated steam, also barely contained, and was forced through channels and tubes to harness the immense pressure.

King John looked out the window at the scenery that flew by. He saw endless Oossah plains that led to black mountains in the distance. John was still amazed at all the progress his people had accomplished. Magick was a power rising in the west, but John had seen the marriage of magick and steam for himself, and he was admittedly apprehensive. The night terrors only occasionally invaded his restless nights.

He reached over to his wife and smiled. The jab of emotion he felt in his heart could result in no other reaction. That Snow could sleep so peacefully with the noisy train jostling and occasionally releasing pressure via steam whistle was a testament to her clear conscience. He reached tentatively to her swollen belly, and the next generation of Oossah rulers. He felt the gentle rise and fall as Snow breathed. He thought he felt a kick or punch from fists and feet still forming, but he was never sure. Snow repeatedly would grab his hand and place it here or there, and declare that the baby was doing somersaults. The mental image of that always made him smile.

They were returning from a diplomatic meeting with the neighboring kingdom, Rookskye. The King of the Rook had a new advisor, and in a display of forward thinking, this advisor was a woman. She claimed to have future sight, and her dire warnings of armies marching across the lands and soldiers more brass than men had brought images back from the depths of his memories. In fact, he thought he had seen his old tutor, Reese, in the Rookskye castle.

He closed his eyes and watched her die that day on the mountain. In his waking hours, he felt a twinge of shame that the memories of his tutor and savior had faded so. Snow shifted under his hand, a quiet snore escaping her lips. He smiled at the thought of the most beautiful woman in all the land doing something so pedestrian as snoring.

His smile deepened. With the magic mirror destroyed, he wasn't even sure Snow was the fairest of them all. It mattered not to him, though; he was so in love with the woman he was tasked with killing, and their unborn child, that physical beauty was just not important to him. He saw her for her real beauty: *compassion*. The people adored her not for her appearance, but for her heart.

Soldiers walked down the aisle quietly, but with a precision he had come to know from the Royal Guard. At the same time, he felt the train slow, the endless pitch of steam pistons suddenly lowered. The pressure on his ears lessening as the train slowly glided to a stop. His guards gathered at a window and pointed in the distance.

~

FALLING...

Snow couldn't overcome the sensation. It was as if she were a bird, and strange forces conspired to ground her.

But I do not wish to be grounded!

She labored to spread her wings, but something kept them tucked against her delicate body. She struggled against her bindings, but they held true.

"Please let me fly," she sobbed.

"Queen White!"

Snow opened her eyes and saw concern in the eyes of an old man. His eyes showed no color, but she could tell this man had lived a significant portion of his life in darkness.

For a blind man, he displayed a remarkable grasp of his environment. When her eyes opened, he smiled, his ruddy cheeks and white whiskers doing the emoting his eyes should have.

"I was blind long before you were born, my Queen."

"I did not..." she started, and took a deep breath to settle the noise behind her eyes, and the flashes in her ears. After the hypnagogic cloud had cleared, she continued. "Apologies, sir, I appear to be out of sorts."

"Sir?" The man whispered and looked off into the distance.

Snow considered that she used phrases and assigned actions a sighted person would, and her pale cheeks flushed in embarrassment.

"Do not worry, Queen White," he replied and returned his attention to her. "You are not the first, and you will not be the last."

"How did you-" she started, but he interrupted her.

"Sight is but one of many of our senses, but that is a topic for another discussion."

Snow stretched and rubbed her belly. She hadn't felt the baby since opening her eyes. Her hands instinctively protected the future ruler of Oossah.

"She's fine," the man whispered. "You've been in a fever dream for two days. I may not have working eyes, but I do have The Sight, my Queen."

Snow let out a slow breath, realizing who the old man was. "Are you...?" she asked.

The man bowed deeply. "I am Byangoma, and I have long abandoned my quest for sight."

Snow reached out and touched Byangoma on the shoulder as he struggled to stand. "You need not bow, seer. You consulted my father until that woman terminated your services."

"Ceridwen's puerile heart is a sad story, but I foresaw

all the events leading you inexorably to me at this moment when Oossah needs you the most." He smiled again and grasped Snow's hand gently. "You and Reese will bring Oossah back from this dark time."

Snow's eyes blurred. She was overcome with grief. She squeezed Byangoma's hand, and whispered, "Tell me what has happened."

Byangoma nodded, retrieved a makeshift chair, and began the tale of Ceridwen's pandemic rise to power and the enslavement of the Oossah people. The story lasted through supper. It was the last meal Snow White would eat as Queen of Oossah, henceforth she would be a warrior, her place foreseen in this dark new world.

*R*ennoc Woods grew more oppressive with each step. The tall trees' thick canopy absorbed more and more sunlight as they traveled further along Pelyse's invisible path. Even the once thick bramble had given way to bare, hard-packed ground that jolted them with every step. Sky had only ever known being a soldier, and her woodcraft skills were second to none among the Sisters. She had tracked Tenyks through every terrain Oossah had to offer and was almost always tagged to be an advance scout. So she found the ease with which the Dwarves simply disappeared, even when there was naught but tree trunks for cover, deeply disconcerting.

The only exception was Poedy, who hadn't left her side since they had entered the woods, although he did seem to enjoy Cloud Dancer's companionship more than hers. He walked with the horse's leads in hand, and would gently reach up to pat his neck every now and then. Cloud Dancer had taken years to bond with Sky, and he was usually frightful to everyone else who encountered him, but he had even started to nudge Poedy affectionately after mere hours of marching.

Then Poedy stopped and pulled Cloud Dancer still with him. In only a moment, the other dwarves appeared, each alerted. Sky didn't know what was going on and wasn't about to wait. In a smooth motion, she dismounted with both scimitars out and scanned the tree line, near and far, for whatever was bothering the dwarfs.

"You'll not be needing those yet," Odc grimly said to her. "Our fight isn't yet at hand."

"I must go," Poedy said, surprising her. She had never heard him speak before.

"I know," Odc said, as a single tear disappeared into the tangles of his beard.

Poedy turned and looked at Sky, and she was suddenly glad she had already unsheathed her scimitars. She had never seen Poedy's face show more than simple joy and earnestness. He had never seemed fully to understand the gravity of their situation, nor the consequences of their quest. Now, there was no longer any simpleness to his face. *Nor joy.* Cloud Dancer shook his head in a whiny and pawed at the ground as though a battle approached.

"Poedy?" she whispered, sheathing her scimitars and kneeling in the harsh, scrabble dirt.

"I will miss you," he said with a voice tinged with the kind of sadness that ran too deep for tears.

"He'll be needing your horse, Sky," Odc said, breaking the moment.

"I don't understand any of this!" she spat in frustration. "What is this? What?"

"Hush woman," hissed Prymgu, "you'll wake the trees themselves!"

Before Sky could answer, Poedy took her hands in his. "I am needed elsewhere," he explained. "It is my obligation; my duty; my time. It is far, and time is short.

"It's a safe journey for him," Poedy added, nodding toward Cloud Dancer.

"Pypha?" Sky heard Odc call. "How lays the land?"

"The horse cannot go much further," Pypha reported from his scouting. "It turns into a swamp in a mile. Lung flies, too."

Sky nodded her assent. On impulse, she kissed Poedy on the forehead and was surprised at how cold he was. His countenance didn't change, but he squeezed her hands before releasing them and deftly mounting Cloud Dancer despite his stature. Sky grabbed her pack from her horse, patted his neck and bade him farewell. He replied with a gentle nuzzle and a soft wicker before letting Poedy lead him back out of the woods.

"His fate lies elsewhere," Odc said in response to her unasked question. He raised a hand to stop Sky. "When we are through this I promise I will explain. For now, though, I fear we must hurry."

"Very well, King Odc, though you still owe me more of an explanation for Prymgu's words about my duty."

"I told you all I can. The less you know, the less hesitation there will be. Trust me. Trust your queen."

"I do."

Odc grunted, and the party continued.

"Lung flies?" Sky asked, returning her attention to the journey.

"There," Pypha said, his usual grin gone as he pointed toward a nasty cloud of white specks, lit by the afternoon's slanting sunlight. "We'll need to wrap our heads from now on. They get in your lungs and lay eggs. They won't kill their host, but they don't give a care if they hurt them. Make sure your nose, mouth, and ears are tightly covered."

"Why do I need to cover my ears if they're 'lung flies?'"

"They may not care as much for the distinction as you," he answered matter-of-factly.

Sky nodded, tightly wrapping her head too and descended toward the swamp with the remaining six Dwarven Guard.

~

POEDY PATTED CLOUD DANCER'S NECK IN GRATITUDE. HE would have to go the rest of the way on foot. Time was short; *it always was,* even in its infinite expanse. But, Cloud Dancer deserved more than merely a send off. Poedy gave him a bit of sugar, removed his tackle, and gave him a quick, but thorough, rub down.

"Find Sky, my friend," Poedy whispered to the steed. He watched the horse walk back toward Rennoc Woods, nibbling at the grass as he went. With a wry smile, Poedy doffed his cap to Cloud Dancer's slow retreat and returned his attention to the canyon in front of him. He could see it was a canyon, could see the sharp slopes on either side and the sparse thickets of trees lining the worn, winding path through its narrow fissure, but *only* if he didn't directly look at it.

Although nature's creatures could see the valley, he alone of the intelligent forms was immune to the magick that camouflaged its mouth. Even then, the magick was powerful enough to block him when looked at directly. He walked up to its edge and ran his hand across the illusion, feeling the rough stone: it was cold in the shadows, and warm in the retreating sunlight. Then he closed his eyes and pushed, turning the rock's solidity into that of air. He walked forward, eyes closed in determination until he felt the coarse lines of ancient bark. He snapped his eyes open, inside the hidden valley at last.

~

SKY SCREAMED PRYMGU'S NAME AS HE CRUMPLED TO A still heap at the foot of the brass automaton. This close to the Enchanted Mirror, the automaton's steam reserve never dropped. With its only weakness gone, the Dwarven Guard and Sky fought a futile battle they had already lost. Prymgu's desperate sacrifice had only delayed the inevitable, letting Pelyse and Pypha pull Odc and Lubfash's limp forms away from the automaton's killing blow.

Sky fought to remove her brass scimitar from the soft mud of the bog. Half the blade had been lost in her first thrust at the automaton, its crisp point replaced with a jagged line halfway down the blade. She had already resigned herself to death, and she knew the dwarfs had too. They had battled valiantly nonetheless and refused to concede even while suffering grievous wounds. Sky was all too aware of her own injuries and knew that they had failed. They underestimated the power of the automaton and Ceridwen's dark magick, and they would all die because of it.

"For Prymgu!" she bellowed, holding her broken

sword before her, "For the Dwarven Guard! For my Sisters! *For Queen White!*"

The automaton turned to face her; implacably it waited for her desperate charge.

~

AT THE END OF THE PATH WAS A CRUMBLING CABIN WITH A trail of smoke coming from its rough stone chimney. Poedy opened the crooked front door and walked in without hesitation. Inside was a slender dwarf with half moon glasses and ink smudged throughout his massive, gray beard. He looked up and squinted at Poedy, struggling to place his obvious recognition.

"Hello Poedy," Poedy said.

"How'd you know my name?" the dwarf in the cabin demanded, standing up from the table, and sending a flurry of parchments to the floor. "My books! Now you see what you made me do? Who are you again?" he added distractedly as he picked up the sheafs.

"I'm you," Poedy said. He stroked his smooth chin in remembrance of the beard only the other now wore. "Don't you remember splitting me off? The parts of you that *felt* and *recoiled* from your work. You desired only logic to keep the *Books of Time,* and so you sundered me off. Creating the first, and last, dwarf to not have a beard."

The other Poedy took off his glasses and made a show of cleaning them in frustration. "You'll have to leave. Whoever you are. There is work to do. Yes. Much work. These are confusing times. Very confusing. Good-Good day kind dwarf."

"My name is Poedy. Just like you. If you have honestly forgotten, I'm sure you can look it up in one of your volumes." He gestured to the wall of books behind his flustered other self, each shelf home to dozens of leather-bound volumes.

"I- That doesn't matter. The work. Yes, I must get back to work. Oh dear! Oh dear, oh dear, oh dear! I'm behind! Already. It *calls* to me! You must leave. Yes. Leave. I must get back to work."

"Your work," rasped Poedy, his bare eyes darkened with burning fury, "is done."

He unslung a brass axe from his back, its head, and haft burnished from years of use. The Dwarf at the table held up a feather in an instinctive reflex of protection, but then he panicked as it dripped ink on the parchments in front of him. He was still trying to blot it off when the brass axe rent the desk asunder. Fear washed across his face as he staggered back from his smooth shaved self. "But Time needs me!" he pleaded and sagged to the floor. "I have to track the ripples! The realities are my responsibility!"

"No! You cannot rescue time from itself, any more than you can save time from magick. Time needs no mortal help. You know that. *We* know that. It's why," Poedy said dropping to a whisper, "you had to split everything, *everything*, but logic from yourself, *us,* to keep the ledgers.

"Ask yourself, 'how *did* it happen?' How did you, *we,* split?"

"It was time. Time came and... Time..."

"Time? *Time?* Or *magick?*"

"I-"

"His name was Jarvis. I saw him again. You'll remember too. Soon enough," he said, calmly, but with deliberate intensity. Poedy removed a shard of the Enchanted Mirror and tied it to his axe's head.

The axe swung again.

~

TIME SLOWED AS SKY HURTLED HERSELF TOWARD THE automaton. Each step was a painful struggle by itself to overcome both her wounds and the sticky ground. She could see the dwarfs slumped over their comrades, only just looking up to watch her death. She saw the resolve in King Odc's face and knew that she would not die alone. She saw the faintest of nods from Pelyse and was grateful for the approval she saw it convey. Her sword felt wrong in her hand; foreign in its weight and balance. Knowing she could only thrust, she committed herself wholly to the attack, surrendering any defense. The automaton pivoted as though the mud were solid and brought its arm up and around to block her, even as its other arm was readying an overhand blow to follow.

Then, mid-step, the world went white in a flash. Everything, even her own hands, disappeared from sight into a wash of piercing brightness, only to instantly give way in a snap to abject, blank darkness. She staggered to a stop in a world that had suddenly turned blacker than the deepest dwarf cave. Silence enveloped her, muting even the beating of her heart. The smells of the swamp, and of the battle, evaporated as though they had never been. She couldn't feel her limbs, let alone the heft of her sword.

Then, slowly, the darkness gave way to haze, as if reality itself were groggily waking from a deep slumber. She felt the weight of the sword and the smell of rot. Then, among a tangle of images, the automaton began to resolve. Its armor was blurred, and it was still more mist than metal when she saw, in a fleck of time, it's real face. *Her face.* She stabbed without hesitation, feeling her sword shudder through the Automaton's unprotected neck. It fell to its knees, pulling the sword from her hand as reality sharpened from the haze with a thunderous *KRAACK*

Sky stood over the automaton as it slumped to one side. Sky looked down at herself, her dead form partially encased in brass that hadn't been fully able to form. She shuddered at the pockets of raw flesh surrounded and enmeshed by polished metal. Sky's retching was interrupted by a gentle hand that pulled her away from the vileness.

"The prophecies said that only the queen could kill herself," King Odc said in fast, rasping breaths. "There is more I would have you know before we die."

"*I* don't understand. I see what's before me, but I don't –"

King Odc, panting heavily, held onto Sky's elbow for support. He too looked upon the mangled artifice that was neither machine nor human.

"It is the queen that you look upon."

"It is me that I look upon," Sky argued.

Odc closed his eyes and inhaled. His lips moved as if he were praying silently. His eyes opened, and he turned to Sky. "From where do you hail Sky?" Odc asked the confused Sister.

Sky didn't have the time or strength for this. She wanted to run and tell her queen that the brass automaton was defeated. She wanted to run before her blood ran out, but she felt the eager pull on her hand. She felt the still powerful grasp of the dwarf king, and it made her sigh.

"I'm from Oossah." She declared with great exasperation. "I was born there."

Odc nodded and replied, "So was the Evil Queen."

Sky sheathed her brass scimitars; the broken one required her to complete attention to work the broken blade into its leather scabbard. "That-" She returned her attention to the wounded head of the Dwarven Guard. "That doesn't prove anything."

"What did you do when you were a young maiden?"

Sky crossed her arms over her chest and felt a twinge from her elbow. "I helped my father at the brewery," she replied.

"You were a common girl?"

Sky looked down at Odc. "I guess I was. We all were until the day Ceridwen took the kingdom and our men."

"Yes, yes, but what about after that? Were you married; did you have children; did you continue brewing?"

"I-" Sky started to reply, but then stopped, the words dead in her throat. "I cannot remember," she confessed.

"What *do* you remember?" insisted Odc.

"Fighting," Sky answered. "I remember fighting beside Snow as one of her Sisters." A blush crept across her cheeks. "I remember falling in love with Reese and making love to her." Her face fell with another memory. "I remember the day she went away and the day she died and the day we fought Ceridwen before she escaped." Sky knelt in front of King Odc. "Why do you persist with this line of questioning? We must advise Queen White of the battle."

King Odc placed his hand gingerly on Sky's shoulder. "Those are weak memories, frail and small. It was when you were re-created that day that memories began to form. Before that, this you," Odc tapped his gnarled finger on Sky's chest. "And this," he waved his hand to encompass all that they could see, "did not exist." Odc twined his fingers and stretched, his knuckles making a soft popping sound. His eyes never left hers, and he appeared to wait for a response from the befuddled young woman.

Sky stared at the dwarf king with her eyes wide and mouth agape. Who was she? She closed her eyes and tried to focus on the memories of her youth. They were just out of reach. It was as if they were fish, swimming in a crystal clear pond. The perfect surface of the water bent her sight. Each time she reached for one, she missed and the fish swam away. The analogy was apt since she now felt as if she were drowning in the new information. That couldn't be right, could it? Why would Snow White allow her to fight at her side if she knew what she was? If what Odc had said was true, then Sky didn't want to speak, unless her words unravel more of how unreal she was.

Odc nodded as if he was aware of her train of thought. "You must ride and fetch Snow White. The portal will be ready soon, but you must seek her and call her here for we, I am afraid will be dead soon. I cannot say more now Sky, but soon you will know more. Run now, do your duty."

SKY STUMBLED THROUGH THE FOREST, HER LIMBS WEARY and her body heavy. She ignored her wounds at the hands of the brass automaton. She refused to call the aberration within the metal construct herself. It was easier to hate it if she ignored the possibility that it was she. She hacked and slashed a straight path back to Oossah Keep with her scimitars, no longer caring to look after the foliage that she longed for as a master of woodcraft. She also knew, as a master tracker, that should anyone wish to follow her, she was making their task infinitely easier. But what of it? Did the gods of old care what an echo of hatred and malice did with her abhorrent existence? Was she in some way responsible for Ceridwen's wrath, or the devastation through time caused by the brass automaton? Did she kill Reese, her lover? Could she even atone for the sins of her other self? Her past self? *Her wretched self?* What would happen to her once all of Oossah discovered that she was a fraud?

Sky realized that she had slowed and stopped in the wood while she pondered her new understanding of existence. She propped herself on her broken scimitar and waited for her will to carry her onward. But she *had* no will of her own. She was a piece, a fragment, not a person or a friend, not a lover or a warrior. She was no more whole than one of the magical fragments of the Enchanted Mirror were. Just like that mirror, she was but a shard of her true self. Was she, not unlike those fragmented shards, just a tool to be used as someone else saw fit? These thoughts and so much more stampeded through her head, and for the first time that she could ever remember, she was frozen in indecision.

Lost in these grim thoughts, Sky wept for the second time that day, and her quiet sobs continued unabashed until a soft puff made her look up. Cloud Dancer, unsaddled, prodded the soft dirt with his hooves. Sky offered him a weak smile, sheathed her weapons, tenderly pushed herself up and let her trusted companion carry her to the Keep where she would find Snow White.

~

IT WAS QUIET IN THE BRIGHTLY LIT ROOM, SO MUCH SO that one could hear the dust shuffle in the stale air. An interrupting beam of sunlight snuck inside through a narrow row of windows and cascaded down a large, round mirror. A mirror that didn't reflect anything back. In truth, the room gazed into the mirror, but the mirror didn't gaze back. It was matte, an ashy fog draped over its smooth surface.

A blue jay flew past the windows and descended toward one, landing on its stone ledge. It pecked its feathers clean bathing in the weak warmth of the sun and then began a small chirp. A sudden gust of wind overpowered the serenity of the circular room and a tall construction in the middle of it, huffing and puffing, releasing clouds of vapor began rotating its seven circles, clicking them into a position secured by brass locks. The wind swept the blue jay from its ledge and into the room. It chirped frantically batting its wings against the ominous current existing solemnly inside the transcendental stone area. A purple glow pierced by blood-red thorns began to swirl in the middle of the portal as it burst open.

As Jarvis, Ceridwen, and the automaton stumbled through, the brass construct fell to the stone floor in a spillage of blood and banged old parts, the blue jay was sucked into the carnivorous whirlpool.

Ceridwen pulled herself away from Jarvis and stood above the automaton. Malformed as it was, it was also a mirror image of her current visage: older, but the same heavy, brass vessel in which she resided. She brought an automated hand to caress an automated face without any love or gentleness.

Jarvis sat upon a brass chair, ornamented as would befit a king. He stroked his white beard, gazing into himself more than into the real world and the room.

"What happened, Jarvis, why did we flee? Snow White was in my hands!"

"What happened there indeed, Ceridwen? And no that is not a rhetorical question. How did Snow White know where to look?"

Ceridwen was lost for words.

"Someone must have told her," she finally said.

"Someone?" Jarvis cocked his eyebrow. "Might it be *you* my Queen of Evil that did speak of our plans?"

"Why would I?"

"Sky would," Jarvis hissed at her.

"What would I have to do with a silly little girl?" Ceridwen remembered the face of the young blond, *a beautiful face,* though still common, smeared with the blood of her Tenyks.

Jarvis stood from his self-made throne and walked in front of the mirror, the other beholding him before he called upon it.

"Mirror, mirror on the wall show me the Sky before them all."

Quick to its command the mirror gleamed with the requested image. The girl, Sky, was standing above a shattered automaton bearing her face. The King of Dwarfs, grasping her, desperate for support, mouthed the truth and Ceridwen, close enough to the mirror could hear it. "Only the queen could kill herself."

"These are lies," Ceridwen spoke slowly.

Then King John's former advisor spun and pointed his thin finger at her.

"This is your past, present and future all coalesced into one. I created you a body fit for war, a body that would carry you everywhere through time and help you fight Snow White again and again *and again* until she was defeated so thoroughly that the mirror could see her no more!"

Ceridwen stood toe to toe with Jarvis, her perfect brass nose nearly pressed against his. She was smaller than the wizard, but her brass suit made her more intimidating.

"You promised me a body of armor to please my advances. and when in dire need, armor to lead an army with. You're just an old trickster, *a fraud* Jarvis, and I consumed your lies like hot bread. You turned me into a monster and gave me weak magick; spawning mindless farmers and cattle boys armed against Snow White and her magick, her Sisters, her dwarven friends. You are not to blame anything on me for your *misbehaving* with time."

"I gave you everything you needed to defeat Snow White's pathetic forces. You spent the magick I gave you on your visage and on that huntsman. Your poor choices lead you to a miserable decade in the shadows of a kingdom that didn't love you. I became time itself, fitting the needed pieces so you would win, *always win* and for that, I paid a dear price."

Ceridwen nodded at the mirror, her yellow eyes squinting at the image. "What of this girl then?"

The image of Sky standing above the defeated

automaton sat frozen at the moment showing both their faces.

"You cannot remember all of them, dear Ceridwen. There are so many of you out there, scattered, lost, and forgotten by time. I had hoped," Jarvis said waving his hand to brush away the repeating image and cloud the mirror in gray again, "that all of you would bend to the dark will of the magick, but *no.* I took a leap of faith in your hatred, and it failed me."

"It seems we failed each other, Jarvis."

"No Ceridwen, you don't understand. When we first met, you spoke of your revenge so passionately I was sure nothing could stop you from destroying Snow White once and for all. That's why I took all the risks. But alas, a part of you grew to love her, admire her. One of you wanted Snow White to win and cease the dark magick."

Ceridwen was taken aback. She walked around the room, her brass heels clicked harsh on the stone floor.

"You chance to compare me once more to a filthy peasant, and I will squish you wizard."

Jarvis laughed. "Believe me or not, there was a prophecy as there are many, but this one given to the dwarfs made news of an evil queen and her mirror self, reflected throughout the land using all the mirrors, creating that many more identical images. This nearly immortal queen was set to rule before being murdered by one of her own selves. Prophecies are simply time streams, a future unwritten, only guessed. I tried to prevent much of it, and you nearly *did* succeed in taking out all of Snow White's family. Of course, one part of the prophecy couldn't be erased, and that was the evil queen herself. I predicted a lot of happenings but never did the mirror show me when and which reflection of you would kill the brass automaton of the future. In this, I did fail you."

"*I*n this, I did fail you."

The enchanted mirror flared to life and revealed instance after instance of Jarvis admitting his failure again and again. Ceridwen viewed each missive as the same Jarvis looked upon infinite versions of herself. Each version of Ceridwen she saw was in various states of disrepair. One was even missing an arm. The mirror altar was mostly the same as her reality, but she spied more than one altar room covered in foliage and surrounded by crumbled rock. The reflected infinity in the mirrors caused her head to ache, and she turned away from the constant display of her defeat.

Jarvis put his staff away and clasped his hands behind his back. He walked in wide circles around Ceridwen.

Finally, he stopped, turned to Ceridwen and said, "Snow White once told you, I know this as I saw it in my mirror, 'Her Magick has, and shall, become so dark it mocks the prohibitions of time itself.'"

Ceridwen met his eyes, but no comprehension marred her gleaming features.

"It bothered me for many nights how Snow White would know to say that. Could it be that she chanced upon a guess? Is she that clever, Ceridwen? I think not, for such words don't cross people's minds without a happening."

"A happening?" Ceridwen asked.

Jarvis slowly nodded. "An intrusion. She would know them because she would hear them from me, and that inevitably is the burden you've bestowed upon me Ceridwen. I see that now, but no matter my faults, you are the reason for Snow White's triumph. You have goodness in your heart!"

"No!" Ceridwen screamed backing away from the advancing warlock.

"You feel compassion!" Jarvis spat at her.

"No! Never!"

"Kindness!" He continued his verbal assault.

"I would rather die!"

"Love!" He hissed it like it was a dirty word.

"Shut up!"

"Pity!" The malice he displayed was apparent.

"No more!"

"Fear!" He crossed his arms over his chest.

"Never!" Ceridwen yelled, the steam clouding her vision, beaming her illuminating eyes at Jarvis, who shook at the sight of the augmented woman.

"And yet, unpredictably a part of you was all of the above. You, my Brass Queen inevitably led Snow White to your destruction. Look into that mirror and see your hands helping the Queen win!"

"SHUT UP!" Ceridwen grabbed a hold of the oak staff and swung it against the mirror. The shattering was thunderous, and it brought both Ceridwen and Jarvis to their knees. Jarvis covered his ears as the echoes of time cried in deafening discord. Flying glass cut his wrists and face, and he curled into a ball. The room was lit by crimson light. Ceridwen remembered seeing it somewhere. She remembered holding a brass sphere in her hand and offering it to the gaping red mouth of a swirling newborn portal. The tendrils protruding from the mirror licked her face, and it burned the brass, but she couldn't feel any pain, not physical. It was after all just her armor.

When the cacophony ended Ceridwen counted the glass shards. There was one for each of them, John and Snow, Reese, Jarvis, herself. The rest was granular dust of pointed glass, crunched barely audibly beneath her brass feet.

"What have you done?" Jarvis asked picking himself up off the ground. His face had many cuts.

"I ended your spying. Time cannot be trifled with like this. Living in all these versions and never winning, I don't want that. I made a mistake entrusting my survival to your hands. I won but with an atrocious face and wounded pride. If Snow White comes here to seek her vengeance, I will end her the way I know. She is a stupid girl, eating apples off of stranger's hands and buying ribbons. One last trick she would buy too."

Jarvis clapped his hands. "If you so desire my queen, very well. But before you say another word come."

Jarvis went to the window and peered outside. "Here, behold your kingdom."

Ceridwen stood by him and gazed upon the land beyond the tower of the dark wizard. The rich meadows stretched as far as the eye could see from the Oossah Keep to the smaller villages scattered on the Royal Road. They were barren, rusty gold breaking into dust at the slightest gust of wind. The wind carried little whiffs of smoke, tiny charcoal pieces reminiscent of a still burning fire. In the distance, the forest swayed, naked white trees caught in a perpetual winter that stripped them of their colors. The wild river once silver now ran brown and coagulated.

"A thousand years of bickering and fighting. A thousand more automatons spilling from the debris of time stimulated with the worst in magick. And a land deprived of an actual ruler. That is what not killing Snow White gives you: everyone dead, and no one to behold your beauty. No one to rule over. Now without the mirror, I cannot see which is the truth because this is a land unmasked, a land where there is no magick to conceal it."

Jarvis walked back to the empty mirror frame, leaving Ceridwen to clasp her brass fingers into a mighty fist.

"Now imagine, Ceridwen, if Snow White finds herself here where the mirror is already shattered, where all of you is hidden, not just this mangled imitation from the past, not just you with your yellow eyes, but all of you! She would destroy us both! She would destroy everything you've worked for. You will never be the better while she breaths."

Ceridwen looked down at her hands and imagined them wrapped around Snow White's thin, white neck; she imagined how it would snap at the slightest pressure, Snow White going limp in her arms, with nary a kiss to wake her up this time. An image of her had done them a trick, fooled by Snow White's kind heart and heroine bravado. But now, at this moment in time, Ceridwen knew she was the truest of them all, a vessel of hatred, agony, and betrayal: her absolute evil would soon face Snow White's weak compassion.

"When Snow White comes, she will weep her magical tears for one last time."

Jarvis nodded and began picking up the mirror fragments.

~

HAD ANYONE BEEN IN ATTENDANCE, THEY WOULD'VE heard a sudden intake of breath as lungs deprived of life decided they still had more to give to the cause. They would've also witnessed The King of Oossah throw off a tapestry covering his broken body.

King John dragged his body out of the throne room, his trembling fingers scraping at the hard stone, his broken limbs heavy behind him. John had stopped hearing the battle cries of the Tenyks; somewhere near there were hushed voices and the rough dragging of weaponry to a pile. It was over then, Ceridwen had lost, or perhaps had fled, and his wife was somewhere in the castle busying herself with her Sisters, celebrating or crying. Victory and loss were interwoven here, appearing hand in hand.

It took John hours, or it could've been days to pull his body up the stairs to his chambers. He couldn't quite tell because there were times when he seemingly awoke prostrated on the stairs and began his ascent once again. He thought about Snow in the aggravating minutes before each struggle for the next curving stair. Had she looked for him in the ruins of her kingdom, *their kingdom?* Did she think him dead, or still subjected to Ceridwen's manipulations?

It was dark when John reached his chambers. The room was cold and unlit, but John could still see the tiny glass fragment under his bed. He crawled to it, praying it would still work even after the magic that held him seeped from the smooth surface and dissipated in the air. Finally after clawing at the narrow space like mad, John clasped his fingers against the mirrored shard.

Putting it to his lips, he murmured a wish, *a favor*, for a single glimpse, *the last chance.* Hesitantly, the mirror brightened, and John exclaimed, tears pooling in his bloodshot eyes.

"It's now or never my love, now or never to save us all."

~

As soon as Sky reached Oossah with the Keep looming over her, dark and unwelcoming still, she knew the darkest hour had come. Climbing off Cloud Dancer she caressed his mane, coloring it red for her hand was stained with the blood of her wounds. She bid him a final farewell and paced herself the way a warrior would arriving at long last home and not long now to her dearest. Sky smiled at the thought she would soon see Reese.

~

Snow was standing before the brass throne

studying it with disgust. There was a time when she had sat on that damned thing, proud and happy, listening for the whistle of the steam. John was beside her, a loving man with a handsome face, and little Reese ran freely, climbing on her father's lap and stealing his crown. John's throne had been torn down, for Ceridwen imagined herself to be the only ruler. Now neither of them possessed that title. One, a middle-aged woman pitying the dead while smeared with their blood, and the other a cowardly witch spitting her venom still.

"My Queen, Snow," came a weak call.

Snow turned with a smile, but upon witnessing Sky's state it faded away. She ran down the steps and took hold of Sky just as the other woman rolled on her feet. Snow sat them both down, beside the rubble and the quiet.

"It's just Snow, remember?"

Sky nodded and said, "It is done. The automaton is steaming no more, and the dwarf king asks for you. You were right, though, you were so very right my queen."

"About what?"

Sky locked her swimming gaze with Snow's inflating brown eyes. "There was a girl inside that thing. I think I knew her well, or may have known her *once upon a time.*"

Snow hugged Sky into a tender embrace like a mother might her hurt child. "I know, dearest Sky, I know. I'm so very sorry for asking you to learn it this way, but it had to be done by you. My hand, see, it's not strong enough, nor is my will. But yours always was."

The rasps of breath were long and uneven. Then, "Am I evil, Snow?"

The Oossah queen took her time and steadied her breath. She rocked the body in her embrace, hushing her death. "No, my lovely Sister, my brilliant Sky, you are not. But somewhere someone did something to you that filled your heart with so much hatred it couldn't last and burst into many pieces. Somewhere out there a part of you is still in a jealous rage, and she won't stop until she is the queen of the ashes and we but crunch as twigs beneath her brass feet."

Sky buckled in her arms. *There are so many wounds on her body,* Snow thought. *She will be gone before the next breath.*

Sky struggled when she spoke again, "Snow, if it needs to be done, erase all of me from time. Cease this hateful rule, I beg of you."

"I promise," Snow whispered and a sorrowful tear splashed down on the only noble piece of Ceridwen's dark heart. "I don't know how yet, but I feel that soon I shall, and I promise you, my most trusted Sister, the world will only know the best of you. *This you.* You will not be forgotten, Sky."

Weak as it was, but it was, a smile played upon Sky's discolored lips. "There was a boy, I remember. He kept me in a cell, but then we ran, and he kissed me out of slumber. I wonder what happened to him."

Snow's eyes filled with tears, but they weren't magick. Sky exhaled, a word lost on her lips as her eyes stared unblinkingly. Snow bent to place a kiss on her forehead. She spoke to the fleeing memory, knowing it would hear.

"Tell my daughter I love her."

She laid Sky's body at the feet of the throne and

covered it with her royal gown. Snow knew that the other Sisters would do the body justice while she was gone.

Outside the gates, Cloud Dancer was waiting, shaking his head impatiently. Snow climbed on his back and urged him to run fast toward the forest. Time was precious.

*S*now White, queen of Oossah, rode Cloud Dancer as fast as the overworked animal could go. He stopped abruptly at the same spot where Snow believed that Sky mounted him for her journey back to Oossah Keep.

"Only this far?" she asked the horse, who replied with a whinny.

Snow hopped down and took her collapsible brass spear from the satchel. She gave the horse a brief tap and watched him disappear into the Rennoc Woods.

She walked with caution looking for signs of lurking Tenyks or steaming automation, but nature was alone and quiet. Snow realized she couldn't hear any birds chirping, and her old familiar path seemed less lavish than she remembered.

She passed a grave marked by sticks and rocks. One of the dwarfs must have made the little gravestone, and it was beautiful craftsmanship bearing the dwarven sigils of honor. It had just a single name engraved upon it: "Tobias."

Snow walked along the path. When she reached a spot and knew that no danger lurked, she called out to the dwarfs. "King Odc? Pelyse?"

When she heard nothing in reply, Snow traversed further into the deep of Rennoc Woods where no light shone through the thick crowds of high trees. She saw them at the foot of the active portal, a round structure swirling in a red vapor and spitting demonic hisses. Their beards and boots and belts had turned to stone – arms outstretched, mouths shouting, swords thrusting: The last images of their deaths were forever imprinted in stone. Despite their arguments, Snow had much respect for the merry bunch. She may have been the Queen of the Meadows, but Odc had been the King of the forest for centuries. She placed a kiss upon her fingers and delivered it to Odc's cheek.

"Sleep well guardians of time and magick," she whispered.

Before her, the portal was still wrapped in outstretched tendrils, and below it, lay the automaton. Snow looked down upon a younger Sky's face, but when she kneeled to close her eyes, the magick faded away, and an old woman, small and dry of age was held tightly in the brass prison. Repulsed, Snow pulled back.

She stepped over the prostrate body. With her spear at the ready; with no hesitation; with no time to waste; Snow White stepped into the portal.

THE PORTAL ILLUMINATED, STARTLING BOTH JARVIS AND Ceridwen. Jarvis ran for his staff and brandished it with purpose, pointing it toward the portal.

"Here she comes," Ceridwen purred, as steam rose above her head.

≈

SNOW FELT TORN APART AS SHE CASCADED THROUGH THE portal. Time pulled her in all directions, stretching her skin and her limbs to excruciating pain. She had only to focus on where the Brass Ceridwen was and as soon as she did, the portal at the end of this tunnel illuminated her exit.

Snow tumbled out of the portal still grasping her spear. When she looked up and ignored the bruises, she saw Ceridwen's burning gaze.

"You have nerve to seek me here."

Snow shrugged and stood up. She observed the room and found the Enchanted Mirror in its corner, but it was already damaged. "Whatever it takes to stop you for good, Sky Ceridwen."

"Ha!" Ceridwen laughed. "So you do know. The warlock did not lie. Tell me, Snow White, why did you keep your love for her if you knew she was a piece of me?"

"Because she was a good person, perhaps the only one of your shattered heart. She vowed to stay with me until the end no matter what. But you are not her, and none of your other brass forms were either."

Ceridwen, unthreatened by Snow's edged spear began a slow pace back and forth. "Do you remember how we met Snow?"

Snow White nodded. "You poisoned my father and took the place of my mother."

Ceridwen spat. "I was a poor girl, brought up in the farthest house of your kingdom. My father made brews for the local taverns and sent me to sell it. Have you ever stepped in a tavern? It stinks of urine and puke; the men are dirty and drunk. I dreamt to be in the Keep, to live a luxurious life as the royal family. I imagined how I'd run down the corridors, playing hide and seek with my servants, or how I had my morning meal in the gardens, while my faithful hounds laid beside me. You were but a babe when the queen took to bed, ill. Your father was coming home from a hunt unaware that he would soon be a widower. He passed right beside my house and looked down from his silver steed. He looked at me and smiled. I was a young girl then, but old enough for marriage. He was so handsome, the King."

"You enchanted him," Snow said in a gravelly voice.

"I had to. He loved your mother too much. On that day, I promised myself to be his next queen no matter what. It was a silly thought, but a powerful one. Days passed, and your mother perished. On that day, a cloaked man came to me and told me that he could help me be the Queen of Oossah."

Ceridwen looked at Jarvis and smiled, but her brass mouth twisted it into a grimace. "He told me how to trick your father into loving me. He gave me a piece of mirrored glass and a potion to drink. It was filled with magick that made me the fairest of them all. As I walked through the village, all of the men turned to look at me, men who had ignored me before. I already felt like a queen. Jarvis became the King's advisor and me his queen. I kept King Richard mine with the power of the mirror and took to Jarvis for advice. We ruled the kingdom until you, dear Snow White, became of age and the mirror spoke your name instead of mine. I was so angered one night my magick poisoned him. He was talking about how beautiful his dearest daughter had become. His love for you was stronger than my curse."

Snow kept the tears from running down her burning cheeks. She remembered the day her father died, and her stepmother sent her to the forest with a young huntsman, a year or two older than herself. John was to kill her, but he was kind, and the most handsome boy she had seen, with his golden locks and wolfish gray eyes. The evil Ceridwen tried many times to kill her, but no matter what, Snow avoided death. She and John banished Ceridwen from the kingdom. Many years had passed before she rode back from the Rookskye, a diplomatic advisor to help propel the kingdom to a brighter future. *Oh, how she propelled it,* Snow thought, grinding her teeth.

~

CERIDWEN'S SPONTANEOUS LAUGHTER BROKE SNOW FROM her memory.

"See, you won over me many times, *Queen* White." Ceridwen heaped as much scorn as she could on the honorific. "You destroyed my pride, my power. I hid because I couldn't stand seeing you still so beautiful and myself so ugly. Then Jarvis found me again and offered me one last chance to kill you. What I didn't know was that it would cost me my body. My body was replaced with this one." She waved her brass hand to encompass her metallic form. "It's repulsive but unstoppable."

Ceridwen leaned forward in a puff of steam her hands ready to grab the warrior queen.

"We shall see about that," Snow said and swung her spear.

The tip of the spear scraped Ceridwen's chest, but

she lurched forward and gave Snow a forceful push. Snow fell against the wall, dropping her spear. Dizzy, she reached for her weapon, but Ceridwen had grabbed her ankles and dragged her across the room.

When the brass queen released her, Snow jumped to her feet and lurched at Ceridwen with a battle cry. The brass queen swung her fists at Snow's face, but Snow dodged them and swiftly grabbed the raised hand plucking out pipes that released clouds of steam, and the impotent hand dropped to the dusty floor detached, its clockwork parts moving without purpose.

Ceridwen cried out and clawed at Snow's face with her other hand, but the true Oossah Queen was too fast. Snow seized the moment, grabbing the other hand and performing the same dismantling, leaving it to loll beside the automaton's body.

Snow pushed past the brass queen, kicked off her brass shin, and slid on the smooth floor toward her dropped spear. Once in hand, Snow turned back to the advancing monster.

"Jarvis, do something!" Ceridwen screamed.

The cowering warlock hid behind his throne and observed the battle from a safe distance. He stood tall, pointing his staff toward Snow. He cast a spell, murmuring incoherent words through clasped lips. The staff belched fireballs that Snow narrowly escaped. Spotting the glass fragments that Jarvis held in his other hand, Snow devised a plan. Ceridwen was slowed, and the brass queen fought against the steam clouds still billowing from her disabled limbs.

Snow turned her attention toward Jarvis. Her eyes, aflame with anger and pain, frightened him. She was

116 | MARK GARDNER & D. PAUL ANGEL

determined to end them both. As he prepared another chant, Snow stepped quickly as her huntsman husband had taught her and sliced through the staff in its middle. Its magick broken, an ordinary piece of wood remained in Jarvis's hand.

"Your days of dominance are over traitor," Snow announced. The tip of her spear pierced his chest. Thrusting the body forward, she drove him into the portal, twisting the handle to force the clockwork spear to retract from his body as it dropped freely through the event horizon.

The mirrored shard fell from his flying hands and floated in the space between the vortex and Snow's reality. Attracted by the forces of time, the weak magick drove itself into the body of the warlock who had created it, absorbing his remaining power. Jarvis gasped one last time as the sharp shards pierced his body and his face.

Snow watched them shatter as Jarvis' body did the same, dispersing into time, never to exist again. The portal collapsed on itself, time looping around itself until the gateway was permanently closed. Snow stared at the rubble, her only escape.

"You wench! You've trapped us both here!" Ceridwen screamed.

Snow turned around to face her. "Then neither of us will leave, and Oossah will finally find peace."

Ceridwen charged at Snow, jumping high, propelled by her brass legs.

Snow readied her spear, awaiting the drop.

The brass queen landed mere inches from Snow, the impact knocked the warrior queen off balance. A brass leg shot through the raised dust and kicked Snow in the stomach. Snow bent over, and Ceridwen caught her in the chin with her knee. Snow stumbled backward and missed seeing the reattached hands swing at her with incredible force. The impact threw her head back, and she spat blood. Ceridwen repeated the swing and stuck Snow in the face again.

Ceridwen smiled at the tiny puddle of blood from Snow. "You are not the fairest of them all. I am! I am! I AM!"

Raising her body to smash against Snow, Ceridwen laughed, a choking cry of grating metal. Snow blinked through the running blood from her forehead and saw a chance to swing with full force.

The tip of her spear caught an exposed section of Ceridwen's neck. Not of her brass carapace, but of soft flesh. Snow's spear continued forward, forced by the brass queen's lunge. Ceridwen's yellow eyes went wide open as she stared at Snow's face. The spear made a clean cut removing Ceridwen's head from her body. A body that slumped down in an eruption of uncontrolled steam.

The brass head rolled on the floor preserving Ceridwen's final expression of stunned disbelief.

Snow remained with her spear at the ready, a few inches above the beheaded brass queen. It was just a soulless skeleton of brass now, unable to hurt anyone anymore.

Whether the corrupted magick had been destroyed throughout time, Snow didn't know. She limped toward the heavy door and urged it open with the help of her spear.

~

SNOW WHITE LOOKED AROUND IN DISBELIEF. OOSSAH Keep was busy with preparations of some sort. It was loud, and there was fanfare somewhere in the distance.

"My Queen, have you been training again?" a familiar voice asked. "Look at your beautiful face, all bruised and bloodied."

Snow turned around to meet Daisy. She was dressed in an elegant dress and her fiery hair longer than she ever remembered it being. "Daisy?"

"Well who else my Queen?" Daisy smiled and took Snow's hand in hers, leading her away from the main entrance to the keep.

"I shall send for someone to clean the destruction from your target practice." Daisy reached for the spear still in Snow's hand and twisted the handle, the spear contracting into a loose bundle of brass.

"Isn't that Jarvis's chambers?" Snow asked when they neared the former advisor's chamber.

Daisy stopped and looked at Snow, a concerned frown on her face. "Who is Jarvis, my Queen?"

"He's-" Snow began to say, but a realization washed over her. *There was no Jarvis.*

"And Ceridwen?" Snow asked.

Daisy grasped Snow's head in her hands and examined the gash on her forehead. "Are you quite all right, Snow White?"

Snow smiled, flinching at the pain. "I think I am."

"Come then, Good King John is waiting for you. I've been telling off children again for calling him Good John the Cripple, but they find it fitting, and King John doesn't seem to mind it. He thinks the name would sit well on the books."

"Cripple?" Snow asked carefully as they walked down the spiral staircase.

Daisy nodded and tutted. "From the hunting accident a few years back. Did you bang your head *that* hard?"

Snow shook her head. "No, just checking that all is as it should be, I suppose."

Nothing good comes without a price, Snow thought. Then her heart hammered with worry in her chest. "And Reese, is Reese here?"

Daisy stopped and grasped Snow's hand. "It's today, isn't it, the anniversary of her death?"

Snow turned away from her Sister at arms.

"My apologies Queen White. I question you too much without realizing how you must feel on this day."

Snow allowed the tears to run down her cheeks this time. "It's all right Daisy. Lead me to my husband now."

Indeed, no victory came without a bitter price. The kingdom was safe, but Snow's soul had yet to heal. Seeing John smirk and shake his crowned head at the sight of her, she knew it would take time, but time was all they had now.

AUTHOR'S NOTE

Hey, you made it through to the end! Thanks for reading.

We hope you'll take a few moments to leave a review on Amazon or GoodReads. Although we hope you liked *Brass Automaton* and want to shout it from the rooftops, we'll take any review we can get. Reviews allow other readers to make a decision on purchasing this story. Good; bad; long; or short, each review matters, and we thank you in advance for yours!

RETROSPECTIVE
D. Paul Angel

Before Mark reached out to me to co-author The Brass Automaton with him; I had never done a collaborative work of this level before. The idea of a Terminator/Snow White mash-up was fantastic, and I knew we could take the story in a lot of different directions. Mark wrote the first two chapters, and then he tagged me in to write the next two, alternating until we were done. This pattern didn't just help us build an interesting world; it challenged us to write that much better.

Every time Mark posted a chapter I would have to read it at least three or four times before I could even think of building upon it. Each chapter had multiple layers, and a myriad of engaging details. I would usually need at least a night, if not a week, to really decide on how to build my additions. I would have to figure out which nuggets to enlarge upon, which layers to emphasize, and how much balance to give between developing the characters and building the world. By the time I sat down to write I knew roughly where I wanted to go with each chapter, but was still able to enjoy the ride as everything unfolded.

One of the things I enjoyed the most about writing a mash-up is that it opened the door to uncountable permutations of world building. I'd never built a world with another author before, and I really enjoyed the challenge of putting my own imprint on the world while still incorporating and expanding on Mark's ideas. It was incredibly fun to add the element of time travel to a Fantasy world that already incorporated magick and Steampunk technology.

While I enjoyed helping to create the world, and give new facets to several already well-known characters, the best part was the challenge. Every time Mark and I put up a story it was that much better than the last. I could enjoy each chapter he finished, even while knowing it was a direct challenge to me to do better. It was a friendly competition that pushed me to improve with every chapter.

At the end of the day I am grateful to Mark for inviting me along on this journey through time, magick, fairy tales, and future sci-fi. I'm proud of our work, and know I'm a better writer for it.

~

D. Paul Angel is originally from California, USA. He now lives in Portland, Oregon. He writes, commits photography, and is, most definitely, a *Nerd's Nerd*.

Twitter: https://twitter.com/D_PaulAngel
Website: https://dpaulangel.com

RETROSPECTIVE
Mark Gardner

I've done lots of the flash fiction prompts over at Chuck Wendig's site, terribleminds.com. Back in August of 2015, the weekly prompt was "X meets Y pop culture challenge." Chuck had two lists of twenty pop culture things. Well, I got out my trusty D20 and rolled "Terminator" and "Snow White."

As with all of Chuck's prompts I wrote something, and got a lot of feedback from the regulars that do the flash fiction challenges. Paul liked the story and commented as such on my blog.

I had collaborated with Paul on a now defunct online project, and I was familiar with his writing style and attention to detail, so I asked him along for the ride.

It started out with us trying to one-up each other. Each chapter had to end on a zany cliffhanger. After doing that a few times, we decided it was time to take the story seriously, and work toward an end.

We were challenging each other and had a pretty solid schedule for about four months. We managed to crank out twenty chapters or so. Unfortunately, as it often does, life got in the way. Paul passed the baton in November of 2015, and I completely fumbled it.

Over the next three months, I tried to continue the story several times, but nothing seemed to stick. Fans had moved on to other interests. Paul had his own stuff going on. So I couldn't seem to finish it, and no one cared anymore. I couldn't stand the idea of a story with over 20,000 words written ending up in the proverbial dustbin, so I emailed friend and previous collaborator, Cindy Vaskova, to help me finish *Brass Automaton*.

Cindy, the epic author that she is, slammed out a four thousand or so word conclusion to *Brass Automaton*. My initial plan was to rewrite her ending, expanding and trimming as needed. Well, the best laid plans and all that. Some of her stuff got a rewrite, some I just cut and pasted. Cindy did such a great job with *Brass Automaton*, that when it came time to write the sequel to *Sixteen Sunsets*, I knew I wanted to co-author it with Cindy.

Brass Automaton had its ups and downs, but it was a thrill to work with Paul and then Cindy to finish the darned thing.

It took another four months for Paul and I to rewrite what was on the blog. We had some tense and POV issues to fix, plus a plot hole or two to fill in. Several of our colleagues and friends helped with the editing and proofreading, and the story you hold in your hands is the result.

I enjoyed working with Paul, and hope in the future that we can collaborate again.

～

Mark Gardner lives in northern Arizona with his wife, three children and a pair of spoiled dogs. Mark holds a degree in Computer Systems and Applications and is currently attending Northern Arizona University, enrolled in the undergraduate Applied Human Behavior program.

Twitter: https://twitter.com/Article_94
    Website: http://article94.com
    Amazon: https://www.amazon.com/Mark-Gardner/e/B008LHJVAY/

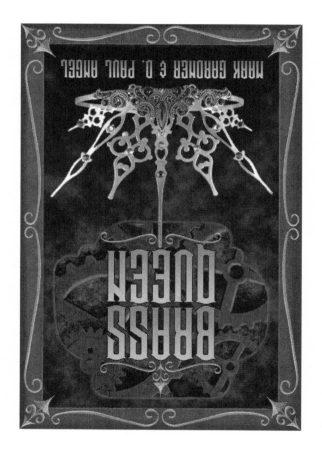

MARK GARDNER & D. PAUL ANGEL

BRASS QUEEN

COMING IN 2018

Clockwork Tales #2